SHARK AMONG THE MINNOWS
PART 1 OF BOOK 1
THE HUNTER/KILLER SERIES
OF
THE FIGHTING TOMCATS

ROSE HILL PRESS, OLYMPIA, WASHINGTON

Shark Among the Minnows is a work of historical fiction and speculation using well-known historical and public figures. All incidents and dialogue are products of the author's imagination and are not to be construed as real. Because of the speculative nature of this work, we have changed some timelines in the present, such as the fact that the aircraft carrier battlegroup depicted in this book has never existed. Also, we have changed the historical timeline in the present to suit the nature of the work. Any resemblance to persons living or dead who are not historical figures is entirely coincidental.

The views presented are those of the authors and do not necessarily represent the views of the Department of Defense or the United States Navy.

DEDICATION

This series is dedicated to the men and women of the Silent Service.

CONTENTS

"Nearly all men can stand adversity, but if you want to test a man's character, give him power."

Attributed to Abraham Lincoln, but the original idea comes from an essay by Thomas Carlyle

"The difference between a good and great officer is about ten seconds."

Admiral Arleigh Burke

CHAPTER 1

KUA LUA APARTMENTS, HONOLULU HAWAII

1315, 12 December, 1990

Lieutenant Commander John Morrison sits barefoot on his couch, wearing only dark blue shorts, contemplating his packed sea bag and drinking a glass of bourbon. Beyond the closed blinds is a peak-a-boo view of the ocean that costs him an extra $100.00 a month. The apartment is clean and tidy and sparsely decorated. Hanging on a hook is a dress blue uniform fresh from the dry cleaners. He takes another sip of bourbon, then looks up as he hears a key turn in the lock of the front door.

A beautiful brunet woman, wearing a green and blue Hawaiian sun dress walks in carrying a bag of groceries. He takes another sip.

Lisa Stevenson asks, "Are you okay?" She smiles down at

 her friend. He's a crazy mix of Japanese and Irish American. His birth parents died in a car accident when he was six months old. He was adopted and raised by his father's best friend, Mitchell Morrison, now a retired Rear Admiral, and his wife, Amanda.

"Yep." Another sip.

She walks into the small kitchen and starts putting groceries away, "Thank you for letting me use your place."

"No problem."

She walks into the living room. "Are you sure you're okay?"

"Yep."

"Do you even hear me?"

He looks at her.

"Oh, John. What's the matter?" She sits and puts a hand on his cheek and turns his face so she can look him in the eye.

A small brief smile, "I don't want to go."

"What? Deployment? Isn't this like your eighth deployment in submarines?"

"Yeah, but this one feels different."

"I haven't seen you for, like, fifteen years. You've changed. Are you always this way before you leave?"

"No." He stands up and walks to the kitchen and refills his glass. "I've never been like this. The San Francisco is a good boat and it is well taken care of. I'm not afraid of it. I just don't want to go." He sits down and his phone rings.

He picks it up, "Morrison."

His CO, Commander George Cumberland, says, "I am having an early dinner at the Hal Koa. Please join me. Oh, if she is here, by all means bring your guest. Is she pretty?"

"Yes, sir, she is."

"Ok. Three then." Cumberland hangs up.

She slides right beside him, "Can I ask who that was?"

"Yeah. That was Commander George Cumberland. My skipper. He invited us to dinner."

"Us?"

"Yep. He wants to know who will be living at my place. He wants to look you over and decide if he approves. That and talk shop. You will be bored out of your mind."

"What's he like? Do you like your skipper?"

"It doesn't much matter if I do or don't. It is a command performance, but you can beg off if you want."

"John. I've set at tables while boring old farts talked to death the minutiae of music they know nothing about. I can handle an old sailor. If you have to go, I will join you."

"Ok." He takes another sip.

She says, "You know you dodged a question. Do you like him?"

He looks her in the eye, "He is brand new on board. He started out as an intense, mercurial ass but he knows his job, and I don't have to like him to work for him."

"Is he the reason you don't want to go?"

"No. I...I don't think so. It is just a feeling."

"You once said your birth dad was Irish. Did he have the gift?"

"Lisa, What gift?"

"I've read that some among the Irish still have the druidic gifts. Maybe your dad had it."

He chuckles, "Lisa Stevenson, are you telling me you believe in supernatural hocus pocus?"

She laughs, "No, but some people do and I know I don't have all the answers." She puts an arm across his shoulders, "When Ted left me, I didn't know what to do. I needed a break from my life. When your mom suggested coming here it seemed perfect. Am I screwing things up by being here?"

"No." He looks her in the eye. "Look, you're beautiful, smart, and kind. Ted was an idiot. My Mom always liked you and she is no doubt trying to match make. I don't know if we might have some kind of future, but I don't think that is what's bothering me."

"When do we have to be at dinner?"

"Three."

"That early?"

"Yeah. Like I said, a command performance. If you don't want to?"

"I'll go. Is the place far?"

"No, just down on the beach at Waikiki."

"Well then, sailor. There is time for you to get laid before we go."

He chuckles, "I'm unattached, remember. What are you saying?"

"I need it too."

He is surprised, "I didn't think you... Really?"

She takes his glass from him, sets it on a table, stands and takes his hand. As they walk to the single bedroom she asks, "Can I do something about the look of this place. It looks like a monk lives here."

"A monk does."

She smiles and pulls him toward the bedroom, "Not anymore."

CAPTAIN'S QUARTERS, K-322 KASHALOT, AKULA CLASS RUSSIAN SUBMARINE

35 MILES SOUTH OF PEARL HARBOR,

1325, 12 December, 1990

Captain, First Rank, Vlad Popov, the submarine's skipper lays fully dressed on his bunk reading 'Hunt for Red October' by Tom Clancy. He chuckles, "Captain Ramius, you are such a fool. I would not misunderstand something so simple as range."

A knock at the door and his executive officer, Captain Second Rank, Yuri Lebedev pokes his head in, "Sir, we are in position."

"Come in, Yuri."

"Yes, sir." He enters the small cabin and closes the door. "What do you read, sir?"

"It is a submarine book written by an American insurance salesman. He is astute in some things, but his Ramius is a fool."

"A Russian in an American book? So, this Ramius is a buffoonish villain?"

"No, worse. He is a traitor to the motherland. It is impossible for someone so foolish to be given command."

"There was the Potemkin, sir."

"True, but that was a junior officer. Not a commander. They give his reason as being the loss of his wife and distrust of his own government to handle advanced technology. He evidently trusts the Americans more."

They both laugh.

"Where did you learn to read American?"

"English, Yuri, and it was in command school, and then a tour in Britain. It was a colleague in Britain who got me this funny novel."

"Thank you for sharing it, sir."

"Of course. Yuri, I need you to learn English as well. Now that the wall has fallen, we will need to interact with the Americans more often. For now, we play the game."

NAVY EXCHANGE, PEARL HARBOR NAVAL STATION
1332, 12 December, 1990

MM3 Karl Gustaf is wandering around the store looking for stuff to bring on Pac. He already has candy, cards, new head phones for his Walkman, and a few CD's.

A pretty lady walks up to him, "Can I help you?"

He briefly meets her eyes, "Nope, your already married."

"I mean with your purchases." She smiles.

"I deploy tomorrow on my first cruise."

She looks at his cart, "I don't see any books. Do you read?"

"I have like fifteen on the boat already but there are never enough books."

She leads him to the book section, "What ship are you on?"

"Boat. The San Francisco."

"My husband is on shore duty. He was on a cruiser. I

thought boats were put on ships."

"Yeah, but submarines are always boats." He looks at the books and sees a familiar title: "'Talon Sword.' God, I had a roommate in prototype who was crazy about this book. Absolutely bonkers. I'll get it."

"I've never read it."

"It is science fiction. It's about a time machine out in Australia that brings a bunch of people from now to World War II. It is a good read. My roommate was convinced the machine was real."

"I'll get it for my husband. It is more up his alley."

KUA LUA APARTMENTS, HONOLULU, HAWAII

1410, 12 December, 1990

The water steams up the translucent doors of the shower they are sharing. He shuts off the water and kisses her again.

Opening the door with one hand, she wraps her other arm around him, "Baby, that was a good, um, shower."

He picks her up like she was a child and steps out of the shower onto the matt.

"John, you're so strong."

Another kiss, "You're...Lisa, you're just wow."

"We got to get ready, honey. Wow back to you."

BARBERS POINT NAVAL HOUSING, OAHU HAWAII

1416, 12 December, 1990

EM1 Stan Wankowski sits in a lazy boy chair with a lap board and papers. His 13-year-old son, Andy, sits on the couch with his 10-year-old sister, Stacy. His wife, Ruth is sitting in her own Lazy Boy. Their youngest, four-year-old Luke is on the floor playing with Lego's.

Stan asks, "Ok, what's your order of march?"

Andy says, "I am the warrior. I go first."

Ruth, "I'll take up drag, so our elf wizard is in the middle."

Little Luke says, "Mamma's character has a beard."

Ruth, "Of course she does. She's a dwarf."

Luke asks, "Andy does your knight have a beard?"

Andy says, "He isn't a knight. Knights ride horses and serve a lord. I walk and serve myself."

"Oh."

Stan says, "Alright. The terrain is rather rocky and arid. There are scrub brush and grass struggling to survive. The hills are rugged but climbable. The old caravan path is worn from centuries of travel. Ok Groo, roll."

Andy says, "Dad it's Groofius the wise." He rolls a twenty-sided dice, "Four."

Luke asks, "How do you know he's wise?"

Andy says, "Because he's still alive."

Stan says, "You see a solitary man walking toward you up the trail. He has a large two-handed sword over his right shoulder, a dagger at his side and a large pack on his back. He has a neatly trimmed grey beard and he is walking with a bit of a limp." Stan rolls a die, "He looks up and sees you."

Andy says, "I say, 'Guys, there is a warrior coming up the road.'"

Luke asks, "How do you know he's a warrior?"

Andy says, "He has a sword."

Stacy says, "We have fought, like, umpteen monsters and stuff to get this far. If this guy is alone, he's tough."

Andy says, "He might be lucky?"

Ruth says, "In your dad's game? No, he's tough."

Andy says, "We're tough too. I just continue walking toward him. There's enough room to meet on the trail, right?"

Stan says, "There is. Is that what you all do?"

Heads nod.

"Ok, when he gets close, he says, 'Howdy folks.'"

Andy says, "My warrior says, 'Howdy stranger. I am Groofius. This is Aeroli. This is Gronk.'"

"Pleased to meet you. Now, I hope you folks aren't

headed up to the Shadow Hills. There is a Gygax up there and it is really pissed off."

Andy and Ruth start laughing. Ruth says, "A Gygax, dear?"

Stacy says, "I don't get it."

Ruth answers, "Gary Gygax was one of the creators of D&D, dear."

"Oh." Stacy says. "Aeroli asks the guy, 'Who are you and what is a Gygax?'"

Stan says in character, "My name is Robin of Thedes. A Gygax is basically a Great Wyrm without wings. They aren't as smart as Dragons but they are really quick. Why would you go after a Gygax?"

Ruth asks, "Why did you, sir?"

Stan says, "The venom of the Gygax is worth a fortune in Tiburnia."

Andy asks, "Do they kidnap people?"

Stan says, "Ah, a noble venture. I'm sorry folks. The larder was further down the cave. I did hear voices so some of its prisoners are still alive, but your friend has probably been eaten. Well, take care."

Andy asks, "Dad, why didn't he rescue the people?"

Stan says, "Ask him."

"Mister, why didn't you rescue the prisoners?"

Stan answers, "What do you take me for? A Paladin. No, not I. 'Twas female voices and women are nothing but trouble. Especially those stupid enough to get caught by a Gygax."

Stacy says, "But, the crown princess of Muldoony was captured. The Queen is offering a huge reward."

Stan says, "Huge reward eh? So, what does a green bunch like you consider huge?"

Andy says, "Her hand in marriage. Royal estates. Titles."

Stan says, "Baa. Have at it then. A title won't feed you or keep you warm at night. Good day to you." Stan continues, "The old man walks off."

CHAPTER 2

KUA LUA APARTMENTS, HONOLULU HAWAII

1430, 12 December, 1990

John puts on his freshly cleaned dress blue uniform. He is wearing four rows of three ribbons below his submarine dolphins. Lisa walks out of the bedroom, wearing a beautiful blue wrap dress, strap heels, and pearl ear rings and necklace.

"Wow. That is nice. You look incredible."

"Thank you. You're looking good, too. What do all the medals mean?"

"These are ribbons, the medals clank when you walk. Highly annoying."

She smiles, tilting her head. "Got it. What do they mean?"

He points, "This one is a merit badge for making my bed nice…"

"Come on, John. At least the top three."

"Ok, this one is the Defense Distinguished Service Medal. I received it for a classified thing I did when I was on the SUBRON-14 staff in Holy Loch, Scotland."

"Classified?"

"Yeah, not earth shattering or anything. Well, it was important. A lot of what I do is classified. Are you okay with that?"

She thinks about it, "When your upset, worked up, or pissed off can we work out a code? I don't need to know why. I just want to be able to help you."

"No code needed. I can say the day sucked, just not always why."

"Ok. What is the next one?"

"This is the Meritorious Service Medal. I earned this as the engineer on the Albuquerque. We commissioned the boat without any incidents and ahead of schedule."

"A big deal that nothing went wrong? That's scary."

"We count the most minor thing as an incident. A sailor screws up his logs and that is an incident. On submarines we have to."

"Ok, love. The next one?"

"This is the Joint Service Commendation Medal. I earned it on the Parche. It is a spook boat and I got it for a spook thing."

"What's a spook boat?"

"Um. We did special stuff that people in suits needed us to do. It is a part of my career that has to be totally secret."

"Ok. Then you can keep my secrets too, right?" She puts her arms around him.

He smiles, "If you like."

She kisses him, "I love you, John Morrison. I always have."

"I love you, too."

WAIKIKI BEACH, HI

1442, 12 December, 1990

LCDR Greg Backes and his wife Carol are walking down the beach with their young son between them. The two pick up the boy by the arms and swing him back and forth as he giggles.

They set him down and he says, "Daddy, why do you have to go?"

"My boat is deploying, son. When it goes, I have to go."

The little guy starts to cry, "It ain't fair."

Greg squats down to face him at eye level, "Your right, Travis. It's not fair. But it is my duty, son."

Travis still crying, "But why?"

"Son, the poet Lovelace wrote, 'I could not love thee so much, lov'd I not honor more.'"

"Honor sucks daddy!"

"It does. It certainly does. Do you know what is worse than honor?"

"No."

"Not having honor."

"Ok."

Carol says, "I think our honorable son deserves some ice cream."

His eyes light up, "Ok, mommy."

WATERFRONT HOME, AINAHOU STREET, MAUNALUA BAY, HI

1445, 12 December, 1990

ST3 Leroy Guthrie is laying on his back in a King size bed with three naked young women. Lorna, the homeowner is curled up on his right, "Leroy, do you have to go?"

"I do, Lorna Love."

Chrissy on his left says, "If you stayed here, we could keep you so happy."

"Oh, darlin' your awesome. All of you are so awesome. I'm a sailor. Sailors go to sea. I have to go."

Debby who is sitting on his hips as they make love says, "Oh, God Leroy. I need you to stay. I'll go through withdrawals."

He smiles at her, "I'll miss all of you too. I love you three."

HALE KOA NAVAL RESORT HOTEL ENTRANCE,

WAIKIKI HI

1454, 12 December, 1990

As John and Lisa walk through the huge concrete and brick planters to the entrance Lisa asks, "What is this place?"

"It is a resort owned by the Navy. Sailors and Marines come from all over the world to vacation here."

As they speak a young family of four leave the hotel in shorts. The two kids are trying to run ahead as mom and dad try to keep them corralled. The mother smiles at Lisa with a weary look.

She smiles, "So, it's a sailor hang out."

"Yeah, kind of."

They turn into the restaurant area and a hostess asks, "Party of two?"

John says, "We're meeting Commander Cumberland."

She says, "You're Commander Morrison and guest, right this way." She leads them through the tables to one overlooking the gardens with the ocean beyond.

Cumberland is also in dress blues. His sleeves have the three stripes of a full commander. He stands to greet them. He ignores Morrison and looks at Lisa, undressing her with his gaze.

John, bristling, schools himself and says, "Commander Cumberland, Lisa Stevenson. Lisa, my skipper, Commander Cumberland."

Cumberland smiles, "A pleasure." Then, "You are correct Commander. She is quite beautiful." He pulls out a chair for her to sit, "Are you enjoying Hawaii thus far?"

Lisa smiles, giving Cumberland a measured look, "Yes. It is so good of John to give me the opportunity of an extended break from my life."

A waiter comes up, giving them menus and taking their drink orders.

Cumberland, nursing a cocktail asks, "John told me you're going through a divorce?"

"It's final now. I should have never married Ted. It is what it is."

Cumberland says, "It seems to me this Ted is the loser when the two of you split. You are quite lovely."

"Thank you. It is fortunate as it turns out that we never had kids. Divorce is so hard on children."

Cumberland's face tightens, "Yes, it is." He lets out a breath and smiles. "So, how did the two of you meet?"

John says, "While I was enjoying a weekend away from Power School. Me and a few of the guys were hanging in Chinatown in DC and she had escaped her brother's concert at RFK." He looks at Lisa, "How is Andy?"

"He is still playing keyboards with Metalsmith. They have a new album coming out soon. He gave me a copy for you."

Cumberland asks, "What is this 'Metalsmith? A band?"

John, "Yes, sir. They play heavy metal. I doubt you have heard of them."

Cumberland, "I haven't. Are they successful?"

John says, "They put out her song, 'Watching Baby Walk Away'. It was one of their most popular."

Cumberland, "Yes. I recall that song, but I thought it was country?"

Lisa says, "It was covered by Carley Woodsen."

Cumberland, "That's right. I have heard it. A rather sad break up song. I would have thought it was made for country."

She smiles, "It is a good fit."

Cumberland, "So, you are one of those heavy metal, punk, hate your country types."

QUARTERDECK, USS SAN FRANCISCO, SSN-711

1520, 12 December, 1990

TM2 Scott Kichiro, a short, stout Guamanian, turns to look at a seagull munching on a muscle then at TM3 Evan Trindle, "What the fuck are you doing on here. You got seven hours before you have to be here."

"Dude. I got nothing to do. Guthrie is screwing every available chick on the island and I can't afford to get drunk."

He digs out his wallet and hands Trindle a twenty, "Go get a beer at the E-club and drink it for both of us. Stay there and watch the sun set, cause you ain't seeing another for months."

"Ok. Don't have to tell me twice."

MMC James Giblin finishes climbing out of the boat, "That's a good thing you did, Kich. How are you doing."

"Ok, chief. I'm going to miss this place."

"We all are. Have you called your family?"

"Yep. Last night."

"You didn't wake them up?"

"Nope. They live on Guam."

BARBERS POINT NAVAL HOUSING, OAHU HAWAII
1535, 12 December, 1990

Stan says, "Ok, as you enter the cave you can hear the rhythmic breathing of the Gygax. The breathing is slow and so large you can feel the air move."

Ruth asks, "Can I see it?"

"You see its tail. The rest of the body is around a corner. What is your order of march?"

Andy says, "Same. Remember dad, I have the blind

fighting feat."

"I know."

Stacy says, "Dad, remember that dragon amulet I found?"

"I do."

Stacy continues, "I'm going to create a magic orb so we can see in the dark. I want it to float above and behind us. Then I pull out my dragon amulet and invoke it."

"Ok. Luke, you're up."

Luke puts down his Legos, "My turn?"

"Yep."

"I fly over to these guys and land where I don't squash 'em."

Stan says, "You're big but not, so big as to crush them."

Stacy, "Wait? What is Lucas doing, Dad."

Stan says, "He is playing his character just like you." He turns back to his youngest son, "Describe yourself, Luke."

"I am a blue-eyes-white dwagon and I'm the king of the dwagons."

Stan and Ruth exchange pleased smiles as his brother and sister laugh.

RESTAURANT, HALE KOA NAVAL RESORT HOTEL,

WAIKIKI HI

1540, 12 December, 1990

Cumberland looks at Morrison and Lisa and asks, "How many songs have you written Miss Stevenson?"

"Twenty-nine that were released."

Cumberland, "I would think that would make you financially stable?"

"Um, yes."

"Then please tell me why you needed to borrow an apartment?"

Lisa says, "Sir, it was more about meeting John again."

"But, he leaves tomorrow?"

Lisa, "Yes, sir."

"I see. So, tell me, if you wrote that, 'Watching Baby Walk Away' song. Who is it about?"

Lisa, "Sir, I've always kept that quiet."

"Come now. Why keep it a secret."

Lisa, "It was about John and I breaking up."

Cumberland, "This John? Him?"

Lisa, "Yes."

Cumberland shakes his head, "Well I must say, Commander, this isn't a good look for you. Your father is an admiral. You're a legacy. You can't be cavorting around with a rock star. It looks unprofessional." He looks at Lisa and smiles, "No offense."

Shocked, Lisa looks to the sea silently. There is nothing she can say.

John grimaces and squeezes her hand under the table, "Sir, I keep my private life private."

Cumberland, "Well yes, but it wouldn't do to have a wife in black leather putting on your eagles."

HAILI'S HAWAIIAN RESTURANT, HONOLULU HI

1545, 12 December, 1990

Master Chief Godoy sits in a booth with his wife, Joy, and two daughters Rachel, twelve, and Debra ten.

Rachel says, "Dad, you're going to miss my Christmas concert."

"I know, honey, but mommy will record it."

Rachel adds, "But where will you be when my concert happens? Could you call?"

"I'll be underway, Rachel. We might pull in somewhere for Christmas. If we do, I will call."

Rachel says, "Daaaaaaad. This sucks. I hate you."

Joy says, "Rachel, you do not."

"But why does daddy leave all the time? It's mean."

Eric says, "Listen, Rachel. I know it is hard. I can't say anything to make it easier. I go to sea because I'm a sailor and that is what sailors do. Rachel, my guys need me."

Rachel says, "But daddy, we need you too," her tears flowing.

"I know pumpkin."

Debra says, "Daddy, what if we hide you in the trunk of the car 'til they're all gone?"

He chuckles, "I'll say this, you're creative. Kids, I have to go. It will only be six months and then I will be back." He looks at his wife Joy, "And guys. This will be my last deployment. I'm up for transfer when we get back. How do you all feel about Bremerton, Washington?"

Rachel says, "Doesn't it rain all the time?"

Joy says, "Our friends, the Bonds spent a tour there and really liked it. Do you remember them from when we were in San Diego?"

Debra says, "Uh huh. Mr. Bond gave me airplane rides all over their house. He is big, big."

Eric says, "yeah, he is that. I heard he's deploying with us. His squadron is on the Carrier. Anyway, girls, I need you two to take care of mommy while I am gone."

Still crying, they choke out, "Okay, daddy."

RESTAURANT, HALE KOA NAVAL RESORT HOTEL, WAIKIKI HI

1548, 12 December, 1990

Cumberland puts his fork down on the dessert plate and picks up his napkin, "Commander, I'm going straight back to the boat. You don't have to be on board until 0200, but I suggest you be fresh for the Maneuvering Watch at 0730." He puts his napkin on his plate and stands up.

"Yes, sir."

LONG TERM STORAGE LOT, PEARL HARBOR NAVAL STATION

1600, 12 December, 1990

ST1 Michael Brown locks up his soft top jeep and shoulders his back pack. All his earthly belongings are in the bag and his rack on the sub. He looks at his CJ-5 Jeep with its faded red paint and splotches of primer. The lot attendant is waiting in a van. After a minute he shrugs his shoulders and turns to the van.

The attendant says, "We'll take good care of her for you."

"I know you will. It just struck me. If I don't come back, who besides a Jeep will miss me?"

"Your folks I suppose."

"Died. Car accident five years ago. My sister has her own life with three kids and a crazy husband. It's just me."

"What's wrong with her husband?"

"He's a bomb squad cop. It's a bang-up job."

The old civil servant startled, laughs and says, "Give me your address. The wife and I'll write ya. Watch her though. She will angle to get you hitched."

He writes down the USS San Francisco's fleet APO address, "Thank you. You can tell her I tried that once. Didn't work out."

"Where can I drop you?"

"How about the E-club?"

"Sure."

TIKI BAR ON WAIKIKI
1635, 12 December 1990

A large Hawaiian guy serves Lisa and John their drinks. John's dress uniform is attracting attention and even discrete photos.

John says, "I'm sorry about him."

"John, all he did was tear open the old wound. I was an idiot to turn down all of your proposals."

"We were both young and dumb. I have never wanted to interfere with your career."

Lisa says, "I know. It is just the Navy. It was, well, it is this huge monolithic structure that seems to consume anyone who is different."

"The Navy isn't one thing. Look, I know you have always been uncomfortable with my job, but it is what I do. Lisa, it is my world, and I am actually really good at it. I am on the command track. I'll get my own boat in a few years, enjoy the hell out of it. I won't be a dinosaur like Cumberland."

"When the Navy is done with you, what then?"

"Cumberland is wrong, Lisa. Us being together won't hurt my career. Even if it did it would be worth it to me."

"Do you have a plan B?"

"Most former officers consult or get boring Government desk jobs. My plan B is the other half of my plan A. Marriage, children, a country house with a white picket fence. I would teach somewhere and write books. I hope to also help a song writer do her thing."

"Why didn't you get married?"

"Because you said no."

"I mean to someone else."

He smiles, looking in her eyes, "Because you said no."

CHAPTER 3

PHONE BOX ON SUB WHARF, PEARL HARBOR HI

1650, 12 December, 1990

George Cumberland waits for the call to ring through.

"Hello?"

"Hi Candace, can I speak with Heather?"

"George, it is late and a school night."

"Candy, we pull out tomorrow. Can't you put her on for a few minutes."

"George, you are the fucking captain of your ship. If you wanted to talk to her you should have called earlier. Just as before, she is not a priority to you, so no. Goodbye."

FORT DERUSSEY PARK, WAIKIKI, HI

1653, 12 December, 1990

John and Lisa walk, hand in hand across the grass, returning to his car.

"How many times did I ask?"

"Twelve, so far." She smiles, looking deeply into his eyes.

"Thirteen isn't a lucky number."

"You already know I am not superstitious."

"True." He looks around. There is an older couple in Hawaiian shirts and khaki shorts. The husband is wearing a SLR camera and USMC ball cap, "Hey Marine."

Startled, "Sir, yes, sir?" The Marine couple approaches the two and the Marine gives a crisp salute that John returns. "Sorry, sir. I was being inattentive to my salute."

John smiles, "I'm shipping out in the morning on a submarine. I didn't plan this very well, but I was wondering if you could take a couple pictures of my girlfriend and I."

Sergeant Major Andy Walker (Retired) says, "I would be honored, sir."

"Thank you." He turns to Lisa, takes both her hands to his chest, "Number thirteen." He takes a knee, "Lisa Stevenson, will you marry me?"

"Yes, oh love, finally, yes."

"I'm sorry I don't have a ring."

Rose Walker pulls one off her right ring finger, "Use this, Commander."

He puts the ring on Lisa's left ring finger, then stands

and faces them toward the Marine with his camera.

Andy says, "You're shipping out tomorrow?"

John, "I am."

"We're here on a Marine reunion. Our Chaplain is here too. Do you want to do the deed?"

They look at each other, Lisa says, "We can have another with all our family later."

John to Andy, "Yes, that would be wonderful."

BROW, USS SAN FRANCISCO, SSN711, SUBMARINE WHARF, PEARL HARBOR NAVAL STATION, HI

1720, 12 December, 1990

Commander George Cumberland walks quickly up the brow ramp wearing his dress blue uniform and carrying a garment bag.

The quarterdeck watch passes on the 1MC, "San Francisco, arriving."

The security watch, TM2 Scott Kichiro, a short stout Guamanian salutes, "Good evening Captain."

Cumberland stops, "Petty officer, you have not asked to see my ID."

"Sir, you're the Captain. I know who you are."

"Site the eleventh general order, petty officer."

"To be especially watchful at night and during the time for challenging, to challenge all persons on or near my post, and to allow no one to pass without proper authority."

"You failed to challenge me."

"Yes, sir."

"Fucking challenge me."

"Yes, sir. Sir, may I see ID, sir."

Cumberland presents his ID, "You are on report, petty officer." He turns on his heel and walks to the forward hatch, steps into the tent covering it and climbs down the ladder.

Kichiro is silent as the captain leaves. Once he knows Cumberland is down below, he says, "What a fucking ass hole."

The deck watch says, "At least your restriction will be while we are underway."

"Fuck you man. This is bull shit."

HALE KOA PARKING LOT

1722, 12 December, 1990

LCDR Greg Backes, carrying Travis, is holding Carol's hand while they are walking back to their car.

Carol, "Isn't that your XO, John?"

"It is." They join the two couples, "Hey John."

John spins, "Hi Greg. Lisa, Andy, Rose, this is my Navigator, Greg Backes, his wife Carol, and the tired guy is Travis. Greg and company, this is Lisa Stevenson and Rose and retired Sergeant Major Andy

Walker.

Greg, "Is this the Lisa who is borrowing your place."

"My fiancé, yes."

Carol asks, "Oh my God! When?"

Lisa, "He just proposed to me for the thirteenth time. Finally, I said yes."

"Are you waiting for after deployment then?"

"For the big wedding, yes, but the Master Sergeant has a chaplain friend."

Carol, "Tonight?"

"Yes."

"Ok, we need to rest Travis a bit, but he can be the ring bearer. I know John will want Greg to stand up for him. They have known each other since the Drum."

Lisa, "Drum?"

"Yes, an old Sturgeon class boat. It was a pile."

Lisa, "Oh God. You know what the Navy is about. We were boyfriend and girlfriend when he was on his first ship."

Carol, "Boat. Submarines are always 'boats' and the surface navy has ships, or to these two," tilting her head toward the two officers, "targets."

"I see. Will you be my maid of honor?"

"Of course, honey. What size are you?"

"4."

"I have my wedding dress at home. It is a 6, but it should fit okay."

"Thank you, yes."

"Beach wedding?"

"I'm okay with a parking lot. I just want this man."

Carol turns to her husband, "Baby, you got Travis. We have a wedding to plan. Get in your uniform and get the chaplain to Keawaula beach, it generally isn't crowded and if we hop, we can catch the sunset.

MANEUVERING, USS SAN FRANCISCO, PIERSIDE PEARL HARBOR

1731, 12 December, 1990

LCDR Steve Miller stands in the corner of Maneuvering as the EOOW, LT Frank Sumpter goes through the procedure for starting the reactor.

Commander Cumberland enters and the phone talker says, "Captain in Maneuvering."

Miller says, "Good evening, sir."

"Where are we?"

"We are pulling rods, sir."

"A word." The skipper leaves maneuvering and the Engineer follows him. Among the myriad reactor instrument cabinets Cumberland says, "I've noticed a degree of laxness in the crew. We are about to deploy. We want the utmost of professionalism."

"I agree, sir."

PEARL CITY MINI GOLF

1733, 12 December, 1990

MM1 Mallory hits his ball through the windmill and raising his putter over his head like a dumbbell, shouting, "Yeah! That's how you do it Gustaf."

MM3 Gustaf takes another swig of beer and says, "Watch this, Mallory." Gustaf hits his ball. It bounces off the sides and back to him, not even reaching the wind mill.

Mallory laughs, "Woo. Impressive. Whatcha need is more beer." He pulls a fresh beer from a Styrofoam cooler, opens it and downs half of it in one pull.

"Shit, Mallory, if you keep downing them like that, I'll have to pour you down the hatch."

Gary burps, "That's the idea. I fucking hate submarines."

"Why did you volunteer?"

"Are they still selling that crap? I didn't fucking volunteer. They needed new Monkey Mates when I graduated from prototype. They volun-told every MM in my class. It is only volunteer when they have enough volunteers."

"Why don't you transfer to cruisers or carriers?"

"I never got a silver bullet."

"A silver bullet?"

"Yeah. A gall stone or trick appendix. The kind of shit that gets you medically disqualified from subs without leaving you drinking through a straw the rest of your life." He finishes his beer and says, "Now get your ass through the wind mill. Show me what you got."

"Mallory, why do you need to get drunk?"

"I start every underway hung over because only a drunk or a fool would go to sea on a boat that sinks on purpose."

"I'm not a drunk."

Gary stares at the young man smiling, "Hit your fucking ball."

KEAWAULA BEACH, HI

1810, 12 December, 1990

Someone set up four tiki torches and flowers that framed the alter area for the wedding. John, still in dress blues, is standing up front talking with the chaplain, Commander Gus Nicholson. Gus is a tall, thin black man wearing a black suit with the clerical collar.

Gus, "So, you are alright with an Anglican service?"

"Yes, sir."

"Good, you know, I eloped with my Lee Anne. Her

parents were furious."

"I bet."

"You are planning a second service later?"

"Yes sir, after deployment."

"I have arranged a license through a friend here. To-morrow, I and your bride will sort out the court house and the Navy. You're not the first to do this."

"Thank you, sir."

He nods, "I understand, son. Now, Andy told me you had asked her twelve times. Fill an old man in on the mystery. What was different this time?"

"Fifteen years and, for her, a bad marriage. The first time I asked, I was an Ensign in Nuclear Power School. She was hanging with her brother's band and writing music. She says no, because she didn't want to be Mrs. Ensign. Eleven times, I got essentially the same answer. The last was right before we broke up in 1975. My dad commanded a destroyer and I thought in front of my parents, it would work. She says no, we argued and she left. For fifteen years she has written music and built a career while I have bored holes in the ocean."

"Do I know the band?"

"Doubt it. It is Metalsmith."

"Oh, yeah. I've heard that group. They had the big hit, 'Watching Baby Walk Away.'"

"Yes sir. She wrote that song."

"Who was it about?"

"About breaking up with me."

Greg and Andy walk up with Travis. Greg is in his dress blues with his sword. Travis is in a black suit that is a little small for him. Andy is in nice cloths and his hat.

Gus clears his throat and the hat disappears.

Greg, "They are just behind me. We have music too."

John, "How?"

"Carol knows everybody. She scared up a musician." As he speaks, a Hawaiian with a ukulele joins them.

John shakes his hand and they all get into position. Then Carol, in a beautiful cream-colored dress with a dark blue flower pattern, walks from behind a bush carrying flowers and walks to her spot. The music starts and Lisa, in an elegant white lace wedding dress steps into view. She walks to John, her eyes only on him.

KAHE BEACH, OAHU, HI

1834, 12 December, 1990

ST1 Thurman Thorsen sits on a blanket in the Hakini Mudra yoga pose, with legs crossed and palms together, the light from the setting sun washing over him. Other than his friend, EMC Andrew Hines, who is sitting in a beach chair drinking beer, he is nearly alone on the beach. A boom box is quietly playing eastern music. He breaths slowly and deeply. When he opens his eyes, he sees an older woman joining him in the same pose.

She is wearing loose flowing cotton clothing, "Are you a Upadhyay. You do that pose perfectly."

Thurman, "I am a mere follower."

"I love and live yoga. If I may ask, who did you learn from?"

"Her studio is in Greenwich Village. Her name is Audrea Thorsen, my mom."

Hines smiles, salutes his friend with his beer and goes back to the book he is reading.

KEAWAULA BEACH, HI

1850, 12 December, 1990

Gus smiles, "You may kiss your bride."

John and Lisa kiss as those attending, and even passersby, applaud. The ukulele player strikes up a tune and starts singing a traditional Hawaiian song. Greg and Carol walk a short distance away and Andy stands facing Greg. Greg unsheathes his saber and Andy pulls out a toy pirate sword. The two lift the blades into an arch. As the newlyweds pass under it, Greg gives Lisa the traditional bump on the butt with the flat of his blade.

CHAPTER 4

CONTROL, K-322 KASHALOT, AKULA CLASS RUS-SIAN SUBMARINE

1703, 12 December, 1990

Starshina first class (Warrant Officer) Sokolov says, "Control. I am picking up a distant vessel at 087, two propellers."

The XO, Yuri Lebedev replies, "Understood. Can you classify it?"

"Not yet sir. Recommend new course 180, sir."

Yuri picks up a phone, "Captain, faint contact at 087. Sonar asks us to come to 180 to align the tail."

"180 is a cardinal point. Come to 174, thank you Yuri."

"Yes sir."

THE RUSTY BUCKET, HONOLULU HI

2310, 12 December, 1990

ETC John Barton walks out of the bathroom and one of the bartenders says, "Hey, John." And slides a beer down the bar to him.

"Thanks man." He smiles at his wife, Barbara, and takes the stage.

Lucy Baker, the lead singer joins him, "What the fuck are we going to do for gigs John? We need a bass."

"I told you my boy Joe is ready."

"He's only 17. What does he know from classic rock?"

"Hey. He's my boy, and he is really good."

The drummer, a 23-year-old red haired girl with a blond streak takes her seat and starts playing.

The rhythm guitar joins them, "Yeah, but he is too young for bars. We make money in bars."

John, "He is allowed in bars if he is working. Just don't let anybody slip him booze. Barb would kill you all." He smiles at his wife. "Barb can get him if you want to give him a shot."

Lucy, "Okay. It's cool that we keep using your amps and stuff."

He motions to his wife and she nods and leaves, "Sure." He starts a base riff and they start their set.

Ten minutes later his only son, Joe, joins them. He is stocky with a wild shock of brown hair. John hands over his base and joins his wife. As the band plays, 'My City is Gone' by the Pretenders, Joe rips up the bass track.

John leans over and kisses his wife, "In a year he will be leading them. In two they will have a label."

"You think?"

"I've listened to what he writes. Yeah, he is way better than me."

"Well, old man, do you have the time for a roll in the hay before you have to report?"

He smiles, nodding his head.

KUA LUA APARTMENTS, HONOLULU HAWAII

0022, 13 December, 1990

John dresses in his khaki's. Lisa quietly helping him. "Are you going to be ok, Mrs. Morrison?"

She smiles, "Now, nothing can take my smile. Um, that's a good line, just a sec." She jots it down as he watches. "You know, husband, you are going to be good for the song writing business. People love a sappy love song. Another good line."

"Anything I can do to help, love. Do you think I knocked you up?"

"I hope so, love." She stands and kisses him, "I wrote letters for you. One a week."

"When did you find time?"

"When you were sleeping." She kisses him, "I can stay awake on your love."

"Your amazing."

He pulls closer and kisses her again, and she asks, "Is it time?"

He nods.

SUBMARINE WHARF, WATERFRONT STREET, PEARL HARBOR NAVAL STATION

0055, 13 DECEMBER, 1990

Commander Cumberland stands on the deck of the submarine as the last of his crew report aboard.

Master Chief Godoy hugs his wife and kids and picks up his bags and walks up the brow. He presents ID, salutes the flag post on the stern, and then the quarterdeck watch, "Request to come aboard."

"Granted."

He turns and watches his family drive away, then approaches the Captain and salutes, "Sir, have we started the muster?"

"We have. E-6 and below are aboard. Some are drunk, but they're here."

"Yes, sir." They see the XO's lovingly restored black 1968 Mustang hard top pull up.

The XO gets out of the passenger side and Lisa, wearing a black dress gets out of the driver's side. John gets his bags out of the trunk and dumps them on the ground. She walks into his arms and kisses him.

John, holding her tightly to him, says, "Six months."

"When you get back, I hope to be seriously pregnant."

"I hope that too. Six months."

"I love you, sailor, now go."

John releases her reluctantly, picks up his bags and walks on board. He can see Cumberland on deck staring at him.

Presenting ID and saluting, "Request to come aboard."

The quarterdeck watch, TM3 Trindle says, "Granted. XO, who is the pretty lady?"

"Her name is Lisa Morrison, TM3."

"You got married? Wow."

Cumberland, "Wow indeed. I will speak to you below."

"Yes, sir."

SONAR ROOM, K-322 KASHALOT, AKULA CLASS RUSSIAN SUBMARINE

0123, 13 December, 1990

Captain Popov stands behind his sonar man as Minin explains, "Sir, this frequency line. It looks like rain."

"Yes, I see."

"Well, it isn't raining anywhere else. This must be an American anti-submarine boat. I think it has two propellers, so probably a Spruance class."

"Very good Minin. I am quite impressed. We will duck under the thermocline so your signal will degrade. It is worth it because then there is no way they may hear us."

"Yes, sir."

CAPTAINS QUARTERS, USS SAN FRANCISCO, SSN-711

0125, 13 December, 1990

Cumberland turns on his XO, "Do you mock me? I told you, she is unsuitable. You must be mad. This whole boat is mad. Do you know half the crew reported aboard inebriated?"

"Sir, it is the last day in port. It is what sailors do. The Navy even has a song about it."

"What are you going on about?"

"'On our last night ashore, drink to the foam.' Do you suppose they were talking about drinking milk?"

"Never mind. Also, the quarterdeck watch failed to ask for my ID when I came aboard. He is lax and unprofessional."

"I'll speak to Commander Backes about it. As for your ID, sir, standing orders were to not challenge the CO for ID. He did what we trained him to do."

"I don't like him. If we weren't pulling out today I would have him transferred off."

"I understand, sir."

"That is all. Be in the Conn at 0730."

"Yes sir."

CONTROL, K-322 KASHALOT, AKULA CLASS RUSSIAN SUBMARINE

0638, 13 December, 1990

Captain Popov stands in Control reading a message, "Yuri, it seems we have a new mission. Moscow reports an American carrier group should be somewhere south of our position soon. We are to track it to its destination and send reports of its location regularly. It seems the Americans believe we have lost our teeth. In this way we may bite them, yes?"

The XO, Captain Second Rank, Yuri Lebedev, "It is a glorious mission, sir. Challenging yes, but this crew; this boat. We shall succeed."

"I agree. Will you join me in my stateroom? We should speak of this."

They walk to the captain's stateroom just off of control. Once the door is closed Popov says, "A little theatrical, perhaps, but it ought to motivate the men."

"It was good, Captain. It was good because it was truth. What did the message say?"

"Continue with operation Red Bowl and the date the American's left San Diego."

"Good. Did you finish the novel, sir?"

"I did. Something relevant to consider. The Americans are professional, yes, but they often take foolish risks. This is due to an unearned sense of invulnerability."

"Yes, sir."

CONTROL, USS SAN FRANCISCO, SUBMARINE WHARF, PEARL HARBOR

0714, 13 December, 1990

Morrison walks into Control in his poopy suit; a dark blue coverall with belt loops, name tape, and rank insignia sewed on. The Boatswain announces, "XO in Conn."

Commander Cumberland is already standing at his place behind the periscope platform, "Well, gentlemen, we have a celebrity among us. Tell me Morrison, did Bon Jovi play your wedding?"

"No, sir."

"Well, seeing that you are such a celebrity, I concede the sail to you. Take us out."

"Yes, sir."

Cumberland picks up the mic, "Station the maneuvering watch."

Morrison grabs a hand held radio, loud hailer, and binoculars. With a lookout and phone talker, he climbs up through the hatch, then through the sail, through another hatch to the conning tower. They hook up the phones and settle in. The line detail comes out from the forward escape trunk and hook lanyards to a flush rail, so if they fall off the round deck, they can be pulled back aboard. Preparing to cast off lines is a bit of a dance because they have to keep the lanyards from tangling.

A tug boat and two security RHIB's approach. Morrison on the radio, "Good morning, Manhattan."

The tug captain says, "Good morning to you." By convention submarine names are never used on radio.

Morrison says, "Start the SPM." The small, steerable electric motor and propeller, which is operated by the helm starts up, getting ready to move them away from the wharf.

The tug is securely tied nose on.

Morrison says, "Release the stern lines."

The sailors untie all the lines aft of the sail letting them fall in the water. Line handlers from a sister sub pull them onto the wharf. The tug toots its horn and begins pulling the stern away from the dock. As the stern gains way, Morrison says, "Release the bow lines." The last of the lines fall in the water and the tug adjusts to pull the entire sub sideways, clear of the wharf.

Morrison says, "Engage the SPM." Then, "Line handlers form up."

The men line up in ranks facing the starboard side. As they enter the main channel and come abreast of the Arizona Memorial, he shouts, "Attention." They come to attention. "Hand salute." The men perform a crisp salute. "Two." They all release the salute and go to parade rest. As disgruntled as many sailors can get, no one disrespects the tomb that is the USS Arizona.

When they clear the Arizona, the tug disengages, and Morrison says, "Disengage the SPM. Ahead one third." The powerful screw of the submarine takes over and powering the San Francisco out of harbor.

After the Arizona they relax their ranks, watching Pearl Harbor pass by. Morrison puts the binoculars to his eyes and starts looking for shipping or other hazards. The lookout is doing the same. As they approach Hospital Point on their port side most of the guys start looking for their family. It is a tradition for the loved ones of sailors to wave them goodbye from Hospital Point. John takes a moment to look over the crowd. He sees Guthrie's ladies first, but then spots Carol and Lisa. He rechecks the navigation and then waves at them. Lisa blows him a kiss. As they continue out of the harbor, they are passed by a couple fishing boats. Once clear of the break water they see two F-14's climbing out of Barber's Point Naval Air Station.

KNIGHT 211, CLIMBING OUT OF NAS BARBER'S POINT

LT Samantha "Spike" Hunt rolls left to circle and wait for the C-2 Greyhound to take off, "How is traffic, Puck?"

"Clear, Spike. If I saw something I would say so."

"Sorry. God, it's a beautiful day to fly."

"Yeah. The new jet is nice too."

"Can you believe Papa is letting us have the new birds. Consecutive numbers too."

"It's nice. Sub pulling out of Pearl."

"I see it, Puck. Probably the San Francisco. It is part of our battlegroup."

"Think they would like a fly by?"

Yeah, but we can't. We would be in the flight path of the commercial field."

"Roger."

On the radio, "Puck, Speedy, light aircraft 10 o'clock at 2000 feet."

Spike, "I see it. A bipla...no a triplane. It's the Red Baron."

Puck on the radio, "Speedy, Puck, it is the Red Baron. Keep an eye out for Snoopy."

CONNING TOWER, USS SAN FRANCISCO

0810, 13 December, 1990

Morrison watches the F-14's fly south escorting a C-2 Greyhound. He takes a slow look around. There is no traffic nearby, "Time to close up shop guys."

"Sir, were those Tomcats flying out to the carrier we are deploying with?"

"Probably."

BM3 Todd, the lookout says, "Sir, I kind of wish I had chosen aviation. What they do is so cool."

Morrison, "Yeah, it's sexy, but every job has its disadvantages. Ever see what happens when a person gets sucked through a jet engine? They come out goo."

"Does that really happen?"

"I've seen videos. I also saw a guy thrown 400 feet down the flight deck by a jet engine. Let's go below."

They gather their stuff and climb down through the hatch. Morrison carefully inspects the hatch seals before he dogs each one. As he dogs the hatch into Control, he says, "Last man down, the bridge is rigged for dive."

Cumberland says, "Very well."

Chief Giblin says, "The ship is rigged for dive, green board."

Cumberland, "Fathometer sounding?"

The Fathometer watch reports, "150 fathoms."

Quartermaster of the watch says, "Checks with chart."

Cumberland says, "Very well. Diving officer of the

watch, submerge the ship."

Diving officer of the watch says, "Submerge the ship, dive, aye. Chief of the watch, on the 1MC, pass the word, dive, dive, sound two blasts of the diving alarm, pass the word, dive, dive."

Chief Giblin says, "Dive, dive!" He sounds the diving alarm, "Dive, dive!" He then opens all main ballast tank vents and announces, "Venting forward," then "Venting aft."

Morrison on the scope, says, "The deck is awash."

The diving officer of the watch knows he can now maneuver using the stern planes, and he orders, "Make our depth 200 feet, 5 degrees down." With a bubbling froth of seawater, the San Francisco leaves the normal world and slips into the alien environment of the sea.

ENLISTED BERTHING, USS SAN FRANCISCO, SOUTH OF OAHU

0915, 13 December, 1990

Mallory finishes stowing the happy stuff he brought aboard: porn, lube, hard candy, cookies, vodka, and kool aid to hide the vodka, pictures of his sons, and a few books should he get desperate. It has to all fit in his coffin locker and a small stand up locker. He carefully puts up the iconic red swimsuit poster of Farrah on the top of his rack and a picture of the Tsar Bomba on the back wall. At least he is senior enough to not have to hot rack. Gustaf walks in, "How are you feeling, Mal?"

"Like I'm on a submarine."

"How's that?"

He looks at his friend, "Like shit. But fuck it. This should be my last deployment."

"I was going to ask you about that. If you hate it, why did you reenlist?"

"It was in the seventies. Are you old enough to even remember the seventies?"

"I was born in '69. The seventies were my childhood. For an old man like you, they were peace love and flowers, right?"

"Right. Look, I joined in '72. In '78 it wasn't peace love and flowers. To me, it was stagflation and unemployment. My wife, Sissy, talked me into reenlisting. In '80, she ran off with a fucking twidgit named Edwin."

"I didn't know you were married?"

"Yep. He pulls out a picture of his boys, "John and Tim. They are 14 and 12 right now. They live in California with Sissy and Prissy."

"What does he do? Prissy?"

"He owns a company that makes military and computer grade lasers. He makes, like, 10,000 times my salary. Still, I send child support because I care about my kids. She probably uses it to buy shoes."

"Why did you reenlist the second time?"

"To get off the Albuquerque. I knew the XO there. He was the engineer. The skipper was a nightmare. Morrison was the only good thing about that boat. He got orders to Holy Loch and I reenlisted for orders to S5G in Idaho. About a year after I left, the skipper was quietly removed for cause."

"What did that guy do wrong?"

"God damn your full of questions. We have a whole deployment to talk, and nothing else to do while we are stuck out here. Go work on your quals."

CHAPTER 5

SONAR ROOM, SAN FRANCISCO, SOMEWHERE SOUTH OF HAWAII

1255, 13 December, 1990

The San Francisco glides silently along at 600 feet just above the thermocline with watch team one, ST 1 Brown and ST 3 Guthrie, on watch.

Brown quietly asks, "So, do you plan to marry one of your gals some day?"

Leroy turns red, "Naw. They don't want to get married. They just like me as a friend."

"So, they're in love with the sausage, not the man. I understand..." Throughout the conversation both are studying the waterfall displays in front of them and listening to the ocean outside using headphones on one ear. Mike says, "Con, sonar, surface target bearing 165. Twin screws. I think it is the Long Beach."

LCDR Morrison pushes a button, "What does the computer think?"

Mike replies, "It is still chewing on it." A dot matrix printer turns on. Brown pulls off the page, looks at it, and reports, "Conn, sonar, computer confirms. Long beach is at 165 and a long way from us."

John says, "Roger sonar." To Combat, "Give me a range when you can." He picks up the phone and dials, "Sir, we have picked up Long Beach at 165. Working on the range." After a pause, "Yes sir." To the watch team, "The skipper wants us to run a practice intercept. Commander Backes, your boat."

Greg, "Come to new course 192, continue at one third. Call the tracking party to Control."

Captain Cumberland walks in and the Chief says, "Captain in Control."

Cumberland asks Morrison, "How far away is the Long Beach?"

"Don't know yet, sir. Sonar says distant."

Cumberland nods once then walks into Sonar, "Brown. Give me a guess. How far?"

ST1 Brown says, "The Long Beach is at least sixty miles away."

"That far?"

"Yes sir."

"You're sure?"

"You asked for my best guess, sir. I won't be sure for a while."

"I need your guesses to be close. I'm making decisions based on them."

"Yes sir."

"Carry on." The captain returns to control.

Leroy asks, "He's pissed, Mike, what are we supposed to do?"

"What we're doing. Don't worry about him. Just do your job."

"But Mike, he's the Captain?"

Mike looks from his screen to the junior sailor, "Can he see what is out there?"

"We can."

"But can he see it without us?"

"No. He is blind without sonar."

"Exactly. He's just stressing." Looking back to his screen, "Just do your job and let the officers do the stressing. If you don't focus on what your job is you might miss something that could get us all killed."

"Okay, Mike."

ENLISTED MESS, USS SAN FRANCISCO

1257, 13 December, 1990

LCDR Steve Miller walks to the end of the mess where all off watch engineering department personnel are sitting waiting for training, "I recorded this excellent 60 minutes report on the nuclear accident at Chernobyl." He puts the VHS tape into a recorder beneath the TV and turns it on.

EM1 Wankowski says, "Sir, isn't Chernobyl a totally different type of plant?"

"It is, but there are lessons we can learn."

LT Cutting asks, "Is it in English, sir?"

Wankowski says, "Jesus Christ, sir. It's 60 minutes, not Suzuta Minutski. Of course, it is English."

Miller says, "That will do, Wankowski. There are a few places where they use subtitles." He turns it on and sits down.

As the film starts, they hear, "Tracking party, lay to Control."

Wankowski stands, "Fuck. Didn't even get any popcorn." He heads forward.

CONTROL ROOM, USS SAN FRANCISCO, SOUTH OF HAWAII

1306, 13 December, 1990

The XO stands calmly in his place while the CO paces around the Control room.

FC2 Harold Edwards says, "Sir, we have a range and bearing for Tango one. It is 58 miles at 175."

The Captain turns toward him like a turret acquiring a target, "How do you report that, Mister?"

"Tango One 58 miles at 175."

The Captain says, "Very well. Conn, continue. Backes, report when we are in range or any other target is identified." He leaves control.

The Chief of the Watch announces, "Captain off of Conn."

MM1 Mallory, still a little bleary from the night before, whispers to EM1 Wankowski, "Jesus Christ, man. What a fucking ball breaker."

LCDR John Morrison walks up behind the two, "Gentlemen, the Captain wants us to be a better team. Should we ever be processing multiple targets, succinctness will be important."

Mallory says, "Yes, sir. I get it sir, but does he need to be such an a-hole while he's doing it sir?"

John looks him in the eye, "We all have our ways, Mallory. Just focus on your job."

"Yes sir."

ENLISTED MESS, USS SAN FRANCISCO

1348, 13 December, 1990

As the nukes watch, the spooky Russian music finishes and the 60 minutes episode ends, but the tape isn't done. An episode of Gumby that Miller had recorded over starts. The Claymation character is playing with Pokey the Pony and the nukes roar with laughter.

EMC Andrew Hines, the E-Division chief says, "Oh, Jesus Christ, Commander, you've done it now."

LCDR Miller, sitting next to him as the cartoon continues to play, says, "What do you mean, Chief."

As some of the nukes start imitating the Gumby voice, Hines says, "You're now the Gumby engineer. You're never going to hear the end of it."

Miller pauses, thinking as they hear a nuke using the Gumby voice say, "Gee mom, Poky has a big dick. Can I play with it, mom?"

Miller smiles, shaking his head, "If it keeps them amused that's fine."

Another nuke in a high-pitched voice replies, "Okay, Gumby, but don't break it. That is mommy's favorite toy."

CONTROL, USS SAN FRANCISCO, NORTH OF THE BATTLEGROUP

1350, 13 December, 1990

John nods to the OOD, Backes, and says, "You have the Conn." As Morrison leaves, the Chief says, "XO leaving Control."

John walks to the CO's stateroom, knocks, and when he is acknowledged, he walks in, "Morning Captain."

"Is all well in Control?"

"Yes sir. May I ask a question?"

"Go ahead."

"I've completed my investigation regarding TM3 Kichiro, sir. He was following standing orders, sir. Why do you want to put him on report?"

"Standing orders?"

"Yes sir. You have not changed the previous Captain's standing orders, and one of them ordered the security watches to wave ID checks for you and the squadron leader. I take it you want to change that order, sir?"

"Commander, the order makes no sense. An impersonator could use it to infiltrate my boat."

"Yes sir. I will make sure all watch standers are briefed going forward, but TM3's case should be dropped, sir."

"No."

"I don't understand?"

"XO, I understand you are a legacy. You grew up in the Navy. You should know that the commander can never appear weak or indecisive."

"Yes sir, but not at the cost of unjust discipline, sir."

"I'll not appear weak before the men."

"Yes sir. Perhaps I could put out that I failed to disseminate your change to the standing order. In that way you don't appear to waver and the petty officer will not be disciplined."

"You would jeopardize your own career for some Third Class. You know he would throw you under the bus in a heartbeat."

"Sir, this isn't about his honor, it is about mine. He did nothing wrong and I'll not have him disciplined when he did nothing wrong."

Captain Cumberland looks at him for a long time, "I'll note your error in your record. That is all Commander."

"Yes sir." John leaves. Once the Captains door shuts behind him, he stops and leans against the bulkhead. Slowly, he stops shaking.

CONTROL, USS SAN FRANCISCO

1405, 13 December, 1990

Wankowski, "Sir, did you know the XO got married yesterday?"

Backes, "I was there. She is incredible. She and Carol hit it off immediately."

"Why didn't he invite anyone else? He's alright."

Backes, "There wasn't time, and he didn't want to mess up your last day. Did your daughter finally use the dragon amulet?"

"Yeah. Luke was hilarious. 'I'm the King of the Dwagons.' It was awesome."

TORPEDO ROOM, USS SAN FRANCISCO

1815, 13 December, 1990

Kichiro is doing weekly readiness tests on the four Harpoon missiles stored on racks in the torpedo room when TM3 Trindle joins him, "Dude, I heard about last night. God that's fucked up."

"Just shut up about it. Maybe he was drunk enough to forget it."

"I heard from the yeoman that the XO pulled your record, man. Your fucked Kiche."

Kichiro takes a big breath and exhales, "Fuck that fucking, mother fucking, fuck tard."

His chief climbs down the ladder, "Kiche, the XO wants to see you in his stateroom."

Kichiro hands his tester to Trindle, "Dress uniform, Chief?"

"No, just go."

The chief climbs the ladder after him and when they get to the XO's stateroom the Operations Officer, LCDR Greg Backes is waiting for them. Backes asks, "You okay, Kichiro?"

"Sir, how the fuck am I going to take care of my wife on E-4 pay?"

"Let's see what the XO says first, ok?"

"Yes sir."

They knock, then walk in. With four people in the tiny stateroom it is crowded.

Kichiro goes to attention and John says, "Relax Kichiro. I owe you an apology."

"Sir?"

"The Captain told me yesterday that he wanted the standing order rescinded. I though he meant it for port calls once we were underway and not immediately. You are not in trouble."

"Really, sir?"

"Really. Commander, please put out to all watch standers that all people will be challenged when they come aboard."

Backes says, "Yes sir."

John says, "Chief, TM2, you may go."

"Yes sir." They leave.

John motions to Backes to sit.

Greg Backes sits and says, "What the fuck is this all about? The old man never issued that order. If he did it would have been in the log, John. Also, it would go to the OOD, not you."

"Greg, your guy is out of trouble. That's what matters."

"Really? He was going to bust one of my best TM's because HE didn't do his job. It's bullshit."

"He's the boss, Greg. When you're the boss you can make the rules. Vent all you want in here, but out there remember to keep your opinion to yourself, ok?"

"You know I will. Thank you for going to bat for my guy. He's a good duck."

"Take care of them, Greg. Anything can happen on cruise."

CONTROL, K-322 KASHALOT, AKULA CLASS RUS-SIAN SUBMARINE

1827, 13 December, 1990

Captain, First Rank, Vlad Popov stands behind his watch officers, listening.

Starshina first class (Warrant Officer) Lukyan Isaev calmly says, "Captain, the vessel is USS Long Beach. Of that I am certain. Beyond the Long Beach I detect a four-screw vessel. A carrier or battleship. I think a carrier."

"Good. There will be other surface vessels and likely a submarine. We should see if we may find them."

"Yes sir."

Popov says, "Helm, give me a one degree down bubble. Make our new depth 230 meters. Left 10 degrees rudder, come to 165."

The Helm repeats, "One degree down to 230. Left ten degrees rudder to 165."

"We begin a game our grandfathers played, but ours is the finest submarine in the sea."

CONTROL, USS SAN FRANCISCO

1910, 13 December, 1990

LCDR Miller observes his watch team as they slowly close on the Long Beach.

He hears, "Conn, Sonar, new contact 174, designate

Nimitz class carrier. It is the Carl Vinson, sir."

"Very well."

He picks up the phone and starts to dial.

"Conn, sonar two new contacts. 178 and 181. Two screws. They look like Spruance cans, sir."

"You found the fleet, sonar. Let me know when we have ranges."

He completes dialing, "Captain, Conn, we have picked up most of the rest of the fleet."

Commander Cumberland walks in, "Report."

Miller says, "Sir we have the long beach at 38 miles at 172. Course is 215 and speed is 16 knots. The carrier appears to be a few miles behind her. In front of the Long Beach are two Spruance class destroyers. Probably the Hewitt and Fife."

Cumberland says, "Get me ranges on the other ships."

FC1 Anthony Walters says, "Yes sir."

Miller says, "Sir, request to descend to 700 feet and drop the array below the thermocline."

Cumberland looks over the threat board, "We should be alone out here. Go ahead."

"Yes sir."

Miller says, "Helm, two degrees down bubble, depth 700."

"Two degrees down bubble, aye."

"Very well."

MESS DECKS, USS SAN FRANCISCO

1915, 13 December, 1990

TM2 Kichiro and TM3 Trindle are watching a movie and talking. Kichiro says, "So I'm off the hook, man. Ya know, the captain's a dick, but Morrison, he's alright."

"No mast?"

"Nope. God, I was so worried. We are barely making it in housing as it is. I would have to send Angie back home to Guam."

"You're from Guam? Shit, man. I thought you were from PI."

"No, man. Guam."

"Did you have to, like, change nationalities or something?"

"Come on, man. Are you a fucking idiot? Guam is part of America."

"It's not a state."

"No, dumb ass, it's a territory."

"We have territories?"

"Haven't you ever heard of Puerto Rico?"

"Yeah, it's a country."

"No, God, no. Look, America has territories; Guam, Puerto Rico, American Samoa, and some other islands and shit. We're all Americans. Didn't they teach you anything in school?"

"We had to learn the 50 states and their capitals."

"The Capital of Guam is Hagåtña. It's a territory. We don't have US Senators and our one representative doesn't get to vote but we are still fucking Americans."

"Ok, man. I didn't know."

"Well, now you do."

CONTROL, USS SAN FRANCISCO

1930, 13 December, 1990

After the sub levels out at its new depth, it takes time for the towed array to level off and settle below the thermocline. The Helm and Planesman are talking about the upcoming Superbowl and the tracking team are checking their numbers. The Helmsman asks MMC Jim Giblin, the A-gang chief standing Chief Of the Watch, "Chief, who do you think will win, this year?"

Giblin raises an eyebrow, "It's a fucking game. Millionaires fighting over a ball, while poor people cheer. I don't care."

"Damn chief. That's harsh."

"It's true. The whole fucking thing is bread and games to keep the masses enthralled while the Government steals their money and takes their rights one by one."

Miller smiles, "Don't destroy all his close-held beliefs on the first watch, Chief. You have a whole deployment to destroy his innocence."

They hear ST1 Thorsen say, "Conn, Sonar, submerged contact bearing 084 below the thermocline. Designate Sierra 1."

Miller picks up the 1MC, "Rig the ship for ultra-quiet. Rig the ship for ultra-quiet." He picks up the phone to call the skipper who walks in followed by the XO.

Cumberland barks, "Report."

Miller says, "Sir, submerged contact bearing 084 under the thermocline."

Cumberland goes to the tracking team, "I need to know where it is."

Wankowski says, "Yes, sir. We're working it."

Cumberland turns away and ploughs his way to Sonar, "Thorsen, give me a range and ID."

"Sir, bearing is constant. We are on parallel courses. Her speed is about 10 knots. Single screw. Sir, I can hear coolant pumps."

"Is it one of ours?"

Thorsen raises a hand and the Captain shuts up.

After several interminable seconds Thorsen says, "No sir. It is Russian. Not sure what class."

"How do you know?"

"I can hear its tail. Russian tails sound different. The screw is a little different as well."

The dot matrix printer kicks in and the Captain rips it off as soon as it stops, "Russian. Akula class. New ship. Good, Thorsen. Start building a profile for her."

"Yes sir. Sir, she is following a parallel track and we are headed for the Long Beach."

Smiling, "Thank you Thorsen. It's an excellent find." As he walks back into control, he says to himself, "It's gonna be an excellent cruise." Then to the Helmsman, "Slow to five rpm. Diving officer check trim. Let's bag us a Ruski."

CHAPTER 6

ENGINEROOM SUPPLY LOCKER, ENGINEROOM, USS SAN FRANCISCO

MM3 Karl Gustaf and MM3 Peter Black stand huddled together, an open can of plumber's putty on the shelf in front of them. Karl says, "Dude, you're a genius."

Peter says, "Ya got the bug juice, right?"

"Yeah, right here." He hands over the bag of green powdered drink mix.

A few minutes and he holds up his masterwork, "I present you Glow worm Gumby." The figurine is a good facsimile of the Claymation character.

"Shit, awesome. Dude, what are we going to do with it?"

"Let's put it on Miller's bed."

CONTROL ROOM, USS SAN FRANCISCO

Commander Cumberland watches over LCDR Miller's shoulder as they maneuver behind the Russian boat.

Miller says, "Level off at 800 feet. Maintain 196."

They hear, "Con, Sonar. We still have Tango One. She is maintaining course and speed."

Cumberland says, "Thank you, Sonar. We have discontinued that track."

"Yes sir. I was just saying, sir. It is loud enough that the Russians probably have it too."

Cumberland, "Thank you ST 1." Under his breath he says, "Fucking New York City faggot trying to tell me how to do my job."

Ignoring what the Skipper says, Miller asks, "Sir, what do you think the Russian's are up to?"

"We're at peace. He is just snooping around. Probably wants bragging rights for when they get back to Vladivostok. Something to brag about to the 200-pound Russian whores."

"Yes, sir. When should we radio in to the Admiral?"

"Once we have a good workup and we know what they are doing."

"Yes, sir."

"Conn, Sonar, Sierra one is turning right. Her bearing is merging with that of the Long Beach."

Cumberland says, "Thank you, sonar." To Miller, "Stay on the track. If anything changes, let me know."

"Yes, sir."

As the Captain walks aft, he has to step carefully around the men cleaning the deck on their hands and knees.

MANEUVERING, USS SAN FRANCISCO

Five sailors sit cramped in a small box in upper level just aft of the reactor compartment bulkhead. LTJG Ashland Muldowney, the EOOW, sits, calmly watching his guys. Muldowney has only been on board four months and he is already qualified the boat, EOOW, and is working on his diving officer qual.

ET1 Andy Brown, the Reactor Operator asks, "So, sir, are you ready to do a double back flip with a gainer?"

"I should have my card done today or tomorrow."

The Throttleman a junior EM asks, "Do they really make him jump?"

Brown, "No, dumb ass. I'm kidding. He has to keep the boat trimmed and balanced during maneuvers. If you were actually working on your Dolphins you would know that."

"Jees, man. You don't have to chew me out. I'm working on it."

"Work on it, harder, and you need to learn how to cuss too. No sailor says 'jees'."

"What?"

"Say: Fuck. Shit. God damn. And cock sucker."

"What?"

"EM3 this is remedial training. Say it."

"My mom would be upset."

"Fuck your mom. And I probably would if she was around. Is your mom a good piece of ass?"

"You're sick."

"You need to learn how to be a sailor or the guys will eat you for lunch. Fucking say the cuss words."

"Oh...ok. Fuck, shit, damn, cock, um, cock sucker."

"Say God damn."

"I can't use the Lord's name in vain."

"Oh, Jesus Christ man."

Muldowney says, "EM3, he isn't being an ass to you, he is actually trying to help you fit in. God will understand that you need to fit in. The Good Book says, 'render unto Caesar what is Caesar's. Give the ET some cuss words."

"Um...Yes, sir. Fuck. Shit. God damn it. Cock sucker."

Brown says, "Good. Now use them in a sentence."

The kid is quiet for a bit then says, "God damn it. If this cocksucker don't get out of my fucking shit, I'm screwed."

Muldowney and Brown, startled, look at each other, then howl.

XO'S STATEROOM, USS SAN FRANCISCO

2145, 13 December, 1990

John walks into his stateroom and sits down in his chair. He pulls off his San Francisco ball cap and puts it on a shelf in his small desk, "Won't need you for a while."

A deep clearing breath, then he reaches into his desk and pulls out a bundle of letters, "When did she get the time?"

The top one is labeled, 'First night.' He opens it and reads:

Darling love,

As you slept the sleep of the well laid, I woke with this idea. I've written 26 letters. Open them once a week. I admit some are spicy, but no cheating. Open just one a week. I hope you pull in somewhere and we get a chance to talk from time to time. Even if you can't, know you have my heart. A good line...

I lost you once years ago

To the vagaries of life.

I told you that you had to go,

You walked from my life.

I was a fool to let us part.

I was a fool from the start.

M. L. MAKI

You should know, yes know,
You have always had my heart.

I tried to give my heart away
To another man.
I cast my heart all astray;
It wasn't mine to give away.
Life had another plan.

I was a fool to let us part.
I was a fool from the start.
You should know, yes know,
You have always had my heart.

When you walked back in my life,
I began to breathe again.
I need you need you in my life.
Let me love again.

I was a fool to let us part.
I was a fool from the start.
You should know, yes know,
You have always had my heart.
Yes, you always had my heart.

I love you, my sweet. Kisses love,

Lisa

She had put some of her perfume on it as well, and her fragrance overwhelmed him. He closed his eyes, fighting back his tears.

NUMBER ONE ENGINEROOM, USS LONG BEACH

0616, 14 December, 1990

The Main Engine Watch, MM2 Maki, is slowly walking around his engine with a sounding rod, listening.

His chief, MMC Craig Chandler is also listening, "I hear it Maki. It is a thrum that comes and goes. The Main Propulsion assistant walks down the ladder. Chandler stands, "Sir we have an unusual periodic noise in the main. Can we have sonar listen to it and give us a frequency. Maybe we can lock down which pinion it is."

The LCDR walks to a phone. The phones are in sound isolating booths due to the loud noises of the engine room. After a few minutes, he looks at the mechanics startled, "There's a Russian submarine under us. How the fuck do we get it out of there?"

MM2 Maki says, "I have an idea, sir."

CONTROL, USS SAN FRANCISCO

0630, 14 December, 1990

LCDR Greg Backes walks into Control, "Request to enter and relieve."

Miller says, "Enter."

The two briefly go over the standing orders and status of the boat, then Miller says, "We are following about five miles behind the Akula. It seems to have wound up its tail and it is wearing the Long Beach as a hat."

"Have we notified the Admiral?"

"Captain wants a good recording first. Problem is the Long Beach is so loud you can hear it through the hull if you listen."

"How long has it been under there?"

"About five hours."

Thurman in Sonar says, "Conn, Sonar. Transient. It sounds like the Long Beach is dropping its anchor."

Miller asks, "Is the Akula going to clear?"

"I think so, sir. It is maneuvering violently. I hear cavitation."

Miller says, "All stop." He picks up the phone, "Captain, we have an issue."

When the captain comes in, Miller explains.

Cumberland, "Have you turned over the watch?"

Miller says, "Not yet sir."

Cumberland nods, "Turn over. Backes, maneuver us

clear and call me when you are ready to come to periscope depth. We need to report in."

Backes says, "Yes, sir." To Miller, "I relieve you, sir."

"I stand relieved." To the watch team, "Commander Backes has the Conn."

Each watch team member reports their status to Backes.

CONTROL, K-322 KASHALOT, AKULA CLASS RUSSIAN SUBMARINE

Captain, First Rank, Vlad Popov runs into Control, "What is happening?"

Captain Third Class Dmitriyev says, "Sir, the Long Beach. It dropped its anchor. We had to maneuver clear."

Popov stands, thinking, "You do well." "Sonar, do you hear anything?"

Starshina first class (Warrant Officer) Minin says, "Just now, sir, I hear popping noises. A submarine is changing depth."

"Give me a bearing, please."

"015, sir."

"Very good. We make our course 290."

"Yes, sir."

"Conn, sonar, a destroyer is maneuvering near us. Spruance class."

81

"Very well. We stay calm and maneuver clear." They hear the distinct boo-waa sound of search sonar ring through their hull.

CONTROL, USS SAN FRANCISCO
0812, 14 December, 1990

Backes picks up the phone, "Captain, coming to 150 feet."

The Captain walks in and hands a paper to ETC Barton, "Send this when the antenna is clear."

Morrison walks from sonar, "The Fife is hammering the shit out of our Russian friends, sir."

Captain, "Professionalism, XO." They can all hear the sonar through the hull.

Backes says, "Right standard rudder, clear our baffles."

The captain pushes a button and speaks into the squawk box, "Sonar, any targets near us?"

"No, sir."

"Conn, stay on course, take us to periscope depth. Link the NTDS as soon as possible."

Backes looks at Morrison, his eyebrow raised. Then the XO walks to the raised periscope deck and looks at the captain who just nods. As soon as the sub reaches periscope depth John says, "Up scope." He spins fully around 360 degrees, "No threats, sir."

"Very well."

Barton says, "Message out, sir."

"Very well."

FC2 Edwards, "NTDS updated, sir."

"Very well."

Barton, "Incoming traffic."

Cumberland says, "Very well. Down scope. Make our depth 200 feet."

The diving officer starts passing the specific orders to dive to the new depth.

Barton hands Cumberland the message.

He reads it, "XO, see me in my stateroom." He leaves.

As the captain is leaving, Morrison says, "Backes, that was a well-executed evolution. My compliments to your entire watch team." He follows the captain aft. He knocks, then enters Cumberland's stateroom. He remains standing.

Cumberland says, "Don't fill their heads with praise XO. Men don't improve with praise. You have to nit-pick even the slightest flaw and then they will improve."

"Yes, sir."

The captain hands him the message.

TO: COMMANDER SAN FRANCISCO

FROM: COMCARGRU 6

PROCEED WITH CSG-6 AT 195 SOA 20 KNOTS.

ASSUMING THE CSG HAS BROKEN CONTACT WITH RUSSIAN SUB DETACH AT APPROXIMATELY 10 54'N 146 17'E. PROCEED BEST SPEED TO RECON CAM RANH BAY. REJOIN CSG AT OR AROUND 6 18'N 108 04'E AT 12/22/1990. CSG WILL PULL INTO CHANNGI BAY, SINGAPORE THE MORNING OF 12/24/1990.

RADM REN

COMMANDER

CARRIER STRIKE GROUP 6

Johns says, "So, they want us to sniff out any Russians in Nam. That is doable, sir."

"Have you been in there?"

"Yes sir. Once."

"What is the approach like?"

"Shallow, sir. Getting in there is a bitch. The bottom is sand and there are a lot of fishing boats.

"How would you do it?"

"Come up the channel and sit outside the bay proper. The acoustics are good and the traffic will run right over us."

"Pull what charts we have and figure out how we can get in the bay. I don't want to skylark outside if we could get in."

"Yes, sir."

"That is all."

OFFICER'S STATEROOMS, SAN FRANCISCO

0212, 15 December, 1990

Miller walks into the stateroom he shares with the other department heads. Grabbing a towel and ditty bag to take a shower, he sees an expertly shaped Gumby on his pillow. He stops, then starts laughing. He sets down his bag and carefully picks up the clay sculpture and puts it on his desk. Shaking his head, he walks out to shower.

CONTROL, K-322 KASHALOT, 180 MILES SOUTH OF WAKE ISLAND

0916, DECEMBER 19, 1990

The flow noises of a high-speed run can be heard through the hull. Captain Popov says, "Ahead one third." He pushes a button, "Alexey, your reactor was splendid."

Captain Second Rank Alexey Dragomirov, the Engineer replies, "Thank you Captain. We will have much decay heat for a time as before." This is their fourth sprint ahead as they track the battlegroup.

"Of course. It is understood. Celebrate your department. We will celebrate the vessel if my guess as to where the Americans are is correct." He pushes a button, "Now rig for silent."

SONAR, USS SAN FRANCISCO, 150 MILES SE OF WAKE ISLAND

1004, DECEMBER 19, 1990

Brown, "Are you worried they might find another boyfriend while we are gone?"

"Nah. Mike, that is the difference between what I have and what you want. I don't own the girls. If they want to date that is fine. When I get back if they don't want to get back together it will suck, but I'll deal with it. A wedding ring is hand cuffs for a woman. It is barbaric. You know, like how the father gives the bride away like she is property."

"It's a custom."

"It's a barbaric custom dating back from when women had no rights."

"I'll have to think about that." He stops, hand raised, "What do we have here?"

Guthrie, "The computer thinks it is magma flow. There are old volcanos all over here."

"Yeah, but it just stopped. Let's trace it back."

A few minutes later, "Ok, it seemed to change bearing. It can't be magma." He pushes a button, "Conn, sonar, we may have a distant submerged target."

John walks into sonar, "Whatcha got, Brown?"

Brown scrolls the waterfall back and forth pointing at a faint line that then stops, "I think it is submerged and distant. It just dropped off here."

"Ok, Brown. We are closing that position so keep an eye on it. See if we can find it again. We will call this sierra two."

CONTROL, K-322 KASHALOT, 250 MILES SOUTH WEST OF WAKE ISLAND

1112, DECEMBER 19, 1990

"Conn, sonar, contact bearing 032. It's the Long Beach."

Popov smiles, "Good. The game continues."

CONTROL, SAN FRANCISCO, NEAR GPS COORDIN-ATES

John, standing with Steve Miller asks, "I heard you like Gumby?"

Miller laughs and shakes his head, "I recorded a Chernobyl news report over one of my son's tapes. The guys aren't going to let me hear the end of it."

"It will keep them amused."

"Yep. That is what I'm thinking."

Miller says, "We are at 600, 2/3rds bell, below the thermocline, and we are ready to change course for Cam Ranh Bay."

Morrison nods, "Good. Per the Captain's instructions, let's pop up to periscope depth and give the Admiral a 'ta ta'."

Miller smiles, "Yes, sir. Helm, make your depth 150 feet. Come to new course 268."

"Depth 150 feet. Course 268, aye."

"Sonar, Conn. We are coming up to periscope depth."

"Conn, Sonar, no new contacts."

"Anything from sierra 2?"

"Negative. It may have been magma."

"Very well." The boat's deck tilts up as they climb to a shallower depth. As the water pressure eases on the sub the hull expands. This expansion makes subtle popping and groaning noises.

The XO picks up a phone, "Captain, XO, coming to periscope depth to wave bye. We are ready to head to Cam Ranh."

"Morrison, do not be flippant with me. We are coming to periscope depth to report our intent to depart. Carry on, professionally."

"Yes sir."

They settle at 150, circle to confirm no traffic, then ease up to periscope depth. As they settle the XO steps up to the search scope, "Up scope." It raises up and he does a quick 360-degree sweep. "No traffic. Transmit."

After a bit radio reports, "Admiral Ren sends, 'Continue as ordered. Fair winds and following seas."

John says, "Take us down, Steve."

Miller says, "Down one degree, make our depth 600 feet. Steady on course."

They slowly descend as they depart the battle-group.

CHAPTER 7

SONAR, USS SAN FRANCISCO

1319, DECEMBER 19, 1990

ST1 Brown sits in his chair in seeming meditation. His eyes are open, staring at the waterfall display.

Sitting next to him, ST3 Guthrie is fidgeting in his seat. Guthrie sighs. The battlegroup is in their baffles and the ocean is silent. Well, it is never silent. Somewhere off in the distant dark he can hear whale song. It always seems sad. Like they have lost too many friends. This brings to mind the girls he left behind. Should he marry Lorna? If he did would she force the other two out of their life? He turns to his LPO, "Mike..."

Mike's hand flies up telling him to shut up.

Brown studies the waterfall screen as he listens, "Conn, Sonar, submerged contact, bearing 194. Contact is distant."

John motions for Steve to call the captain as he walks into Sonar, "Ok, Brown, what do you have?"

"It's our Russian friend, sir. I'm pretty sure."

"Okay. We could still hear the fleet if it wasn't in our baffles. Can the Russian hear them?"

"Sir, the Long Beach sounds like a scrap metal truck on a country road. They can hear it."

"Thank you."

John walks back into Control as the Captain walks in from the opposite direction.

"Captain in control."

Captain Cumberland says, "Report."

Miller says, "We have an unidentified submarine at 194 distant. We are working out the range, sir."

John says, "The computer is still crunching it, but Sonar thinks it is our Russian."

The captain stops and is silent for several beats, "Ahead one third. Come to new course 165. Take us below the thermocline."

Miller says, "Aye, sir," and relays the orders.

The captain says, "Miller, get behind him and stay behind him. Call me if he does anything aggressive. XO, with me." He about faces and walks out of control.

CAPTAIN'S CABIN, K-322 KASHALOT, AKULA CLASS RUSSIAN SUBMARINE

The phone rings and Captain Third Class Dmitriyev says, "Captain, it is the Long Beach again. I am sure of it."

"Good. Very Good. Ascertain their course and navigate us ahead of them. Also, do not forget that the Americans have a submarine out here somewhere. Remember, this is a patient game."

"Yes Captain."

CAPTAIN'S CABIN, USS SAN FRANCISCO

John knocks on the door, then enters the CO's cabin, "You wanted to see me, sir."

"Yes. I've noticed you are too familiar with the crew. This isn't a Princess cruise line. It is inappropriate, Commander."

"Sir, I am confused. What do you mean?"

"You know exactly what I mean. I've heard you address subordinate officers by their first name. You do that and they will walk all over you."

"Yes, sir."

"XO, I am trying to salvage your career. These people are not your friends."

"Yes, sir."

"XO, speak your mind."

"Sir, I appreciate the need for professionalism. It is vital. My father taught me that a collegial atmosphere in the wardroom enhances performance. If you recall Admiral Rickover says much the same."

"What are you going on about?"

"Rickover says, 'Human experience shows that people, not organizations or management systems, get things done.' We have to take care of the men sir. If we beat them down, we can't get their best."

"Don't quote Rickover at me. You may be a legacy, but you didn't run in those circles."

"Yes, sir, but the point stands."

"Are you challenging me?"

"You asked me to speak my mind, sir. I completely agree that we need to run a tight ship, sir. I just want to give the men a little room to breathe, and a sense that they can excel here."

"If we excel, they excel. The point is unprofessional conduct from the crew. Did you know our engineering department is enjoying a Gumby craze?"

John schools his face, "Yes sir. Commander Miller informed me. He is not concerned about it."

"NOT CONCERNED! They are mocking their department head. I want it squashed this instant."

"Sir, the men need a means to blow off steam. It isn't meant in disrespect."

"Commander Morrison, I see it as disrespectful. Squash it. Am I clear?"

"Yes, sir."

"That is all."

MESS DECKS, K-322 KASHALOT, NEAR THE

BATTLEGROUP

1619, DECEMBER 19, 1990

Popov is sitting with his crew enjoying a bowl of ice cream, "Seaman Gratski, how are you adapting to life in this fine vessel?"

"The ice cream is good, sir. It is even better that we humiliate the Americans."

He nods, "Yes. Do recall though, those who are our enemy today may become a friend."

"Captain, the government is saving much money by decommissioning ships and dismissing sailors. Is there a place for me in the Navy?"

"It is a fair question and one I cannot answer with certainty. If not, you are learning good skills to use in the oil fields or at a ship yard. There will be work enough, I think. When you seek that job speak of me and I will speak highly of you."

ROYAL ARMY FACILITY, THE AUSTRALIAN OUT-BACK

2141 (1141 ZULU), DECEMBER 19TH, 1941

Stephan Leonard approaches a Royal Engineers General and Dr, Heinrich Heinlein, "Doctor, all is ready. The final capacitor is charged."

"Very good, Stephan, inform the others it is time to come to the control room." He steps up onto a platform containing an electrical console with a mass of gauges and instruments on three levels. He motions to the general to step up on the platform as technicians move into the room, finding their places at consoles facing toward the device. Above the consoles, the window glass reaches toward the ceiling, shimmering with a gold sheen.

Stephan, an electrical engineer from London, takes his place overseeing the others as the projects chief engineer. He can see the readouts for the capacitor bank and generators. Never has this much raw power been discharged.

Heinlein, "Would you wish the honor of throwing the main switch, Herr General?"

Looking out at the device the general steps down from the platform, "No, Doctor, it is your device. The honor should be yours."

"Stephan, open the roof, please." Stephan nods and pushes a button and motors whine to life as the roof rumbles open.

"Gentleman, all gauges reading correctly?"

"Yes, Doctor, all the readings are nominal. The capacitors are at maximum. The skies are clear. We are ready," says Stephen.

"Very well, gentlemen, we look forward to our future." He throws the switch. The banks of capacitors release their energy into the device all at once. Even protected by the Faraday cage of the control room the men's hair stands on end. Static electricity dances over their bodies, and runs around the room in a terrifying display. Only the general does not pass out, and even he must hold onto the console to avoid falling.

CONTROL, USS SAN FRANCISCO

2157 (1141 ZULU), DECEMBER 19TH, 1941

They have maneuvered behind the Russian submarine as it slowly sails a couple miles ahead of the Carl Vinson at 600 feet and 175 degrees.

John, "Steve, the old man wants us to squash the Gumby thing."

Miller, "Why? It isn't hurting anything. The boys need something to blow off steam."

"He considers it disrespectful. We need to squash it." Blue sparks start dancing across the consoles and panels.

John says, "What the hell?" Then, "Everyone, don't touch anything. I got it Steve, go aft."

Miller takes two steps and crumbles to the ground.

When John comes to, he is lying on his left side against the periscope deck. He leaps to his feet looking at their status, "Mind the helm." He sees Chief Giblin on the floor at the dive panel, "Chief! Chief Giblin!"

Giblin, rising from the floor, "What the fuck was that, sir."

"Mind your panel, chief." He turns, "Sonar, status?"

CONTROL, K-322 KASHALOT, AKULA CLASS RUSSIAN SUBMARINE

2157, 19 DECEMBER, 1941

Captain Popov climbs up off the floor where he fell, "Status?" The silence is unsettling. "STATUS!"

The helmsman comes to shaking his head, "Three degree down bubble, sir, correcting."

"Depth?"

The rest of the watch team start waking up.

"285 meters, sir."

"Bring us steady at 300. Make our course 260, ahead flank."

"300, 260, ahead flank, yes sir. Flank ordered and answered."

CHITOSE, HOKKAIDO ISLAND, JAPAN

2157 (1157 ZULU), DECEMBER 19, 1941

Professor Asahi Koizumi teaches Architecture at the Seisa Dohto University. He and his unmarried grand-daughter Fukue are enjoying a glass of wine in his solarium. The lights are out and the stars can be seen above. Air operations at the nearby airbase seem done for the day and the neighborhood is quiet. "You honor an old man with your presence. We should be seeking you a husband."

"I am happy, grandfather. I have you and my studies. It is enough."

He can see blue light reflecting off her face and he looks up. A tornado of blue light falls from the sky, seeming centered over their humble home. He can see the modern glass sculpture on a table inside glow brightly blue and remembers the significance of its origin.

A student who loved British science fiction had created it and gifted it to him, telling him of the novel he found the design in. He grabs Fukue's shoulder and pulls them both to the ground.

LECHFELD AIR FORCE BASE, 20km SOUTH OF AUGSBURG GERMANY

135 (1157 ZULU), DECEMBER 19, 1941

US Army SFC Henry Holmes is walking toward the base HQ as the blue lightning falls. The lieutenant walking with him stops and looks up. Henry, a Ranger tabbed infantryman grabs the lieutenant and dives under a truck. Lt. Victor Olsen is still out when Henry comes to with a start. With years of experience, he stays motionless. As the lieutenant starts to wake, Holmes asks, "You okay?"

Olsen, "Let's get our ass to HQ."

"You okay, sir?"

"Yeah." They climb out as single engine prop planes strafes the field. The two run toward the HQ. Before they have taken three steps, a bomb lands on the HQ building where their boss, MAJ GEN Harding is.

Olsen, "What the hell is happening, Sarge?"

"I don't know sir, but we are mighty exposed." As he looks around, he sees a Marine F/A-18 starting to move, "Come on!" He runs toward the plane.

Olsen, "I thought we were exposed?"

"Shut up. Go to the special ordinance bunker. We need to get it the fuck outa here."

"Why are they attacking us? They're German."

"They're World War II planes, sir. Fucking go."

The lieutenant splits off and runs toward the bunker.

Holmes waves down the F/A-18 and shouts to the pilot, "Over there!" Pointing to the special weapons bunker.

At first, the black pilot looks confused, then nods and turns the plane. As aircraft explode behind them, and the tank farm starts to burn, the Marine's fighter is pulled into an armored shelter. The crew there begin wheeling out ordinance and placing them on the hard points.

Captain Louis "Shot Gun" Mossberg, the pilot, shouts down, "Good call, Sergeant. I'll head for England. You need to get these tech's to safety."

"Yes, sir. They should be fine once we're off the base."

"It must be the Russians in disguise, or some terror thing. These technicians know how to make nuclear weapons. Keep them safe."

"Will do, sir."

U. S. Airforce Master Sergeant Kelly O'Brien hands Mossberg a paper, "Sign custody, sir."

Mossberg briefly looks at Holmes, then signs the paper and tosses it back, "Get clear." The cockpit closes and Mossberg trips his brakes and rolls out of the shelter. The air attack has stopped but he can see a couple WWII gray German armored vehicles across the field. He chooses his taxiway and rolls onto the runway and guns the engines. As he clears the trees on the far side of the field, he can feel the thud of small arms hitting his bird.

NORTH OF NIZHNY TAGIL INDUSTRIAL CITY, USSR,

1657 (1157 ZULU), 19 DECEMBER, 1941

Senior Lieutenant Constantin Romanov is struggling to keep his helicopter in the air. When the lightning came, he was at 8000 feet. Now he is fighting to stay above the trees. "Where the fuck are we, Alexi."

Lieutenant Alexi Zorin, his copilot, "I don't know, Romy. We... fuck." They pass under a railroad bridge "We are north of the field. We have to be."

CONTROL, USS SAN FRANCISCO

Brown, "Conn, sonar, what happened, sir?"

John pushes the button, "I don't know yet. Focus. I need status."

"Roger. All systems seem to be functional."

"Very well. Helm?"

"Helm is responding, sir. We are at 500 feet and…"

"Conn, Sonar, the Russians just kicked it in the ass. They're cavitating. They're turning left. Crazy Ivan!"

"All stop." He pushes a bitch box button, "Maneuvering, Conn, status?"

Miller back in Maneuvering says, "Conn, Maneuvering, all systems seem normal, all bells available. We are working on a diagnosis for what happened."

"Very well."

The Captain walks in, a goose egg forming above his right eye, "Report. Why didn't you call me, XO?"

Morrison says, "My apologies, sir. I had to handle the casualty first. Sir, it looked like an electrical discharge. The engineer is diagnosing it. The Russians just pulled an Ivan. General Quarters, sir?"

"Where is the Russian?"

FC1 Anthony Walters says, "Sierra two steady on course 260, six miles ahead of us, and hauling ass, sir."

"Not yet XO. Stay behind the Russians."

Walters says, "Sir he is off our starboard beam. It looks like he is driving away from us and the fleet."

John, "Make right standard rudder, make our course 262." John walks over to the plotting map and studies it.

Cumberland walks up beside him. They feel the sub rolling as it turns in pursuit. Cumberland says, "He could be looking for distance for a missile shot. That or working himself around for a stern shot."

John says, "Yes, sir. Did they outfit the Akula class for anti-ship missiles, sir?"

"It's the Russians, who knows. I'm going to go aft. Follow them. Also, load tube one and two. Do not flood them, though."

"Yes, sir." He hears a phone talker, "XO, there is a medical emergency in the AMR middle level."

John says, "Understood." He picks up the 1MC, "Medical Emergency, AMR middle level."

CONTROL, K-322 KASHALOT, AKULA CLASS RUSSIAN SUBMARINE

The watch officer asks, "Sir, what happened? What do we do?"

"I don't know Dmitriyev, so we report in."

"Are we at war, sir?"

"I don't know."

"Sir, then we, perhaps should not cavitate."

"You are correct. Left, ten-degree rudder. Ahead 1/3. New course, 105. Come to periscope depth."

MANEUVERING, SAN FRANCISCO

Miller stands behind the watch officer as they troubleshoot the propulsion plant.

The Reactor Operator, ET 1 Andy Brown, "Sir, the Reactor Technician reports power range instrumentation is functioning normally."

The EOOW, LT Craig Cutting, checks the Reactor Plant Manuel on the desk. "Very well." To the Reactor Technician, "proceed to step seven, point two, point one, point three. Test RC cabinet power supply."

The phone talker repeats the order and receives a verbatim reply.

EMC Hines opens the door, "Request to enter as Engineering Watch Supervisor."

Cutting says, "Enter."

Hines says, "Sir, all mechanical systems are functioning normally. Both TG's are on line and functioning normally. Switch gear is in its normal line up with no faults indicated. Washburn is working with the RT. I have no idea what just happened."

Miller says, "I don't either. What do the guys think?"

Cutting says, "If we were at the surface, we would suspect a lightning strike or such. One strange thing, sir, the water dropped three degrees after the event."

"Interesting. Cutting, call forward and see if salinity changed."

"Yes sir."

Hines, "What are you thinking, sir?"

"It is a long shot. Maybe a change in salinity effected our hull conductivity. The electrical system isn't grounded to the hull, which would explain why it was unaffected."

"True, sir." They feel the deck roll and start sloping up as the submarine ascends in a turn.

CONTROL, K-322 KASHALOT, AKULA CLASS RUSSIAN SUBMARINE

2210, DECEMBER 19, 1941

Captain Popov watches the depth gage as the sub slowly shallows out, "Up periscope." The periscope slides silently upward from its well. He flips the levers down and does a quick spin, "No targets. No aircraft. Sea state 4. No shadow should be visible. Transmitting."

> To: Headquarters, Pacific Fleet
>
> From: K-322

Unexplained electrical discharge. All systems on line and functioning normally. Request guidance. Are we at war?

Captain, First Rank, Vlad Popov

AUXILIARY MACHINERY ROOM MIDDLE LEVEL, SAN FRANCISCO

Master Chief Godoy sits on the weight bench as HM1 Vince Novogradic takes his vitals. "Doc, I'm fine."

"COB, you had a nasty fall. You were unconscious for several minutes. You are not fine until I say you're fine. Understand?"

"Doc, is this really necessary?"

"I agree with you, COB. If you stopped whining and cooperated, I could finish and send you on your way."

"If I thought I had a problem, I would say so."

"Squeeze my fingers."

The COB squeezes and winces, opening his right hand. Novogradic looks over his hand.

Godoy says, "Fuck, fuck, FUCK. That hurts."

"I thought you were fine?"

"It's not broken."

"How the fuck do you know, Chief?"

"Is it?"

"You sprained your wrist and broke two fingers. I'm going to need to wrap it for now."

The Captain shouts down the ladder, "Is he okay, Corpsman?"

"I'm evaluating that, sir."

"If he is injured, I need you to write it up so we can send him to the carrier."

"I'll let you know if that is necessary, sir."

"Corpsman, this boat is not an infirmary. If he is broke, get rid of him." The captain continues aft into the Reactor tunnel.

Godoy, "Whatever you do don't kick me off the boat, Doc."

Novogradic looks him in the eye, "Chief, if you need to go, you will go. If I can manage it on my own, I will keep you here. Now where else do you hurt?"

A sigh, "I think I hit my right knee."

"Ok."

CHAPTER 8

MANEUVERING, USS SAN FRANCISCO

Cutting says, "Sir, salinity dropped over 200 ppm."

Brown says, "Sir. If it was static shouldn't our meters been effected?"

Miller, "They should, but they weren't. I've never heard of salinity changing that fast without a change of depth. Even then this is unusual."

The captain invades maneuvering, "What the fuck happened to my boat, Miller?"

Miller answers, "Sir, was any other of the ships effected?"

"I don't know. We solve our own problems, Commander. Kick your boys in the ass. I fucking need an answer."

"Sir, what we know is all systems are functioning fine, but we are in colder, lower salinity water. How that caused what happened, I still don't know."

"Don't fucking stand there. I need answers. NOW!"

"Yes, sir."

On the 1MC, "Captain contact Control." He turns on a heel and leaves.

Miller, under his breath, "Well, that went well."

Brown says, "Sir, all reactor instrumentation and controls check out. What can I do?"

"Don't worry about him, ET1. Just keep doing your job."

"Yes, sir."

Miller says, "I need to get back to Conn. Cutting, get your watch team thinking on this. When you eliminate the impossible, whatever is left must contain the truth."

CONTROL, USS SAN FRANCISCO

2219, DECEMBER 19, 1941

The Captain storms in.

"Captain in control."

Morrison, "Sir, the Russians are climbing to periscope depth. They are reporting in. Should we report in as well?"

Cumberland, "Do you think we are at war, XO?"

"I don't have enough information, sir. That's why I recommend checking in with the Vinson, sir."

Cumberland, "A point. Put together a message, XO."

John hands him a paper, "Will this work, sir."

FROM: COMMANDER USS SAN FRANCISCO, SSN-711

TO: COMMANDER CARRIER STRIKE GROUP 6

REG: ELECTRICAL ACTIVITY

On or about 2157, San Francisco experienced an electrical discharge from the hull. One personnel injury, ENCM Eric Godoy. Thus far, all systems are functioning correctly. Evaluating material status. Evaluating whether medical evacuation is necessary. Please advise."

CDR Cumberland

Cumberland reads through the message carefully, "Add, 'Was electrical event a hostile act?' Then send it as soon as we can."

CONTROL, K-322 KASHALOT

2225, DECEMBER 19, 1941

The chief radio operator, Starshina First Class Misha Goncharov, "Sir, there is no response. Nothing. No carrier wave. Nothing sir."

Popov is silent. "Misha..." He looks around the control room. "My crew, this is highly concerning. It also seems very threatening. Oleg, take us down to 100 meters and maintain a course parallel and away from the Americans. How will they react? I will see the XO and department officers in the wardroom."

FLAG BRIDGE, USS CARL VINSON
2314, DECEMBER 19, 1941

Admiral Ren is sitting in his chair reading reports by red light, and occasionally glancing out into the nothing that is the sea at night.

A radioman walks in, "Request to enter with traffic."

Ren looks up, "Come."

After reading the message from Cumberland, he pulls out a note pad and quickly writes a reply, "Send this to every ship in the battlegroup, son."

CONTROL, USS SAN FRANCISCO

Morrison reads the Admiral's message:

> FROM: CDR CSG 6
>
> TO: ALL UNITS
>
> REG: ELECTRICAL EVENT

All units experienced the electrical event. We have lost contact with higher, and with the Hewitt. The event may be hostile in nature, or due to some sort of natural act. As we do not yet know its nature, I am moving the group to THREATCON DELTA. Take all appropriate measures to safeguard your commands.

> RADM Ren

Morrison says, "Miller, we are now at THREATCON Delta. Please note it in the log and gentlemen, stay vigilant."

Miller answers, "Yes sir. What does that mean regarding our Russian friend?"

"I don't yet know. Sorry, Steve." He goes aft to see the Captain.

He knocks at the captain's door, "Sir, we have a response."

Cumberland quickly reads it, then reads it again, "DEFCON 1." When he looks at his XO, he is smiling.

"Sir?"

"For 45 years, we in submarines have toiled at dangerous, but ultimately irrelevant missions. War. War matters. We have a rendezvous with destiny."

"Um. Yes sir."

CHARGING STATION WATCH, USS SAN FRANCISCO

0032, DECEMBER 20, 1941

MM3 Gustaf asks MM1 Mallory, "Dude, what day is it?"

"I don't know. What does it matter at sea?"

"Mallory, it matters. Well, it might. What day is it?"

Gary picks up the sound powered phone and asks Maneuvering. "It's 20 December, Gustaf. What gives? Did you forget to send a Christmas card?"

"No, man. Have you ever heard of a book called 'Talon Sword?'"

"No, you know I don't read the shit that you do."

"You don't read at all."

"I do."

"Yeah, drink menus. Anyway, my roommate in prototype was just nuts about the book."

"So? Come on, get to the point."

"The story was about this time machine. The thing was, the guy who wrote the book based the story on this time machine that was actually built in the desert somewhere in Australia."

"There ain't no time machine in Australia."

"It's there. The thing is, my roommate built one of the antennae for the machine, and 19 December 1990 was the date it was supposed to work."

"So?"

"So, he is stationed on the Carl Vinson. That's our carrier, right?"

"Yeah. Mother fucker. Are you saying he brought this antenna thing with him?"

"Where else would he put it?"

"I don't know. Up his ass sideways."

"It could explain all the lightning and stuff."

"Ok? I didn't read the book. What has happened to us?"

"The thing didn't work in Australia when he discharged it. The thing is, they discharged terawatts of energy and nothing happened."

"Ok, then it's just a coincidence."

"No. Mallory, what if the stuff couldn't move back until the discharge date was reached?"

"Move back. What the fuck are you talking about?"

"Dude, if the book wasn't fiction, it is now 1941. December 20th, 1941."

"Oh, fuck you."

"I'm serious, dude."

"Look, even if your right, you best shut the fuck up about this. Let the officers figure it out themselves. You don't want to be the guest of honor at a court martial."

CONTROL, USS SAN FRANSISCO, TRAILING THE KASHALOT, NW OF THE FLEET

1234, DECEMBER 20, 1941

Morrison is standing with his friend LCDR Backes, "Do you think there is any possibility that a temperature and salinity change could account for the electric discharge?"

Shaking his head, "It is a long shot down here, but

the surface ships experienced it too. I don't think we know enough."

"I agree, and it is concerning. We can't prepare for what we don't know."

Brown in Sonar, "Conn, sonar, transient. New submerged contact designate sierra 3, bearing, 185. Submerged contact flooded tubes."

Morrison, "Call the skipper." John walks into Sonar, "What can you tell me, Brown?"

"Not much. It is dead slow. Sir, it sounds odd for a sub, but it is a sub."

I-7 JUNSEN CLASS JAPANESE SUBMARINE,

1816, DECEMBER 20, 1941

Commander Hirotaka Chiba could not believe his luck. The largest American carrier he had ever seen, and it isn't even zigzagging. The I-7 has six forward firing tubes, but no stern tubes. He just has to wait as this monster ship steams right into his firing solution.

"Open doors for tubes 1, 2, 5, and 6. Set depth to 20 feet."

CONTROL, KASHELOT, NW OF THE FLEET

Minin, "Captain, a transient for certain. A submarine flooded tubes."

"Is it our American?"

"Negative, Captain. A new contact. It sounds a bit like a 613 boat, but different. Two screws for certain."

SONAR, USS SAN FRANCISCO

Morrison is standing behind the sonar operators, "Can you give me a guess, Brown?"

Brown, "Sir, it is moving very slowly. If it were not for it flooding tubes, I may have missed it. There are some odd sounds. This here, look. It sounds like a wire or cable in the water. At first, I thought it might be a tail but it is moving too slow for a tail and the bearing is right on the boat. It's old sir. Two screws. At periscope depth. Maybe a third world boat?"

"Keep on it. We need to know who it is."

"Sir, they're opening doors."

Morrison turns and rushes back to Control.

CONTROL, K-322 KASHALOT

Popov, "Flood tubes. Keep the doors closed. Sonar, I really need to know the identity of the new Contact."

"Yes, sir. It is not in our database. It is not Russian."

I-7 JUNSEN CLASS JAPANESE SUBMARINE

Submarine fighting is a patient job. The amount of

time needed to load and fired torpedoes forces patience. Commander Chiba mumbles, "Haste leads to death, and worse, failure." Then loudly, "Stand by to mark bearing."

"Yes sir," says Petty Officer Sato Nishimura.

"Distance is 36,000 meters. Set torpedoes to slow. I want them all down the same bearing. They will spread enough on the way."

"Yes sir, setting torpedoes to slow," repeats the phone talker.

"Ready. Mark."

"Bearing 312, Commander, "says Sato.

"Bearing 312. Set. Commander", says the Firing officer Chief Isidro Hataki.

"Fire 1, 2, 5, and 6."

"Firing 1, 2, 5, and 6," the sub shudders as compressed air forces a slug of water to expel the torpedoes, one after the other. Four deadly Type 93 Long Lance torpedoes are speeding at 35 knots toward USS Carl Vinson.

CONTROL, USS SAN FRANCISCO, NW OF THE FLEET

As Morrison enters Control from Sonar, "Conn, Sonar, torpedoes in the water. Say again, torpedoes in the water. Sierra 3 fired at the Vinson. The Russians are flooding tubes."

The XO picks up the 1MC, "General Quarters, General Quarters. All hands man your battle stations. Tracking party to the Conn." To the Combat operators, "Flood tubes 1 and 2. Do you have a snap shot for me?"

"No, sir."

The Captain storms into Control, waving the BM1 off as he announces him, "What?"

John says, "New contact, bearing 137, just fired four torpedoes at the Carl Vinson. The Russians are flooding tubes. I've ordered one and two flooded."

"Conn, Sonar, there is a Mark 46 in the water targeting sierra 3."

Cumberland pushes a bitch box button, "Torpedo, Captain, Status!"

TM2 Kichiro pushes his button, "Almost there, Captain." After a moment, "Conn, torpedo, tubes one and two are flooded. Doors are shut."

Cumberland, "Fucking Kichiro. Why is he there?"

CONTROL, K-322 KASHALOT

Starshina First Class Minin shouts, "Torpedoes in the water!"

Captain Third Class Dmitriyev says, "Calm. Status of tubes one and three?" He picks up a phone, "Torpedoes, sir."

Minin says, "The torpedoes sound odd, sir. Four of

them, I think, fired at the Americans."

Captain Popov entering Control, "Leave the tubes flooded, do not open doors." He walks to the chart and Dmitriyev and Captain second rank, Yuri Lebedev, join him.

Minin says, "A fifth torpedo. It is pinging. It is targeting the unknown submarine."

Popov points, "This submarine. Whose is it? No word. We may be at war."

CONTROL, USS SAN FRANCISCO

Brown, "Conn, Sonar, the Benjamin Stoddert fired the ASROC. They are driving between the fish and the Vinson.

The torpedo consul operator says, "Fish are spun up and data is cross checked. Sierra 2 is five miles away. Sierra 3 is out of our range, sir."

John, "Very well."

Backes is studying the tracking map as the GQ watch standers relieve.

Cumberland looks at the two officers, "The Captain has the conn."

The watch standers acknowledge.

Cumberland, "Open doors. Jesus Christ man, hurry up."

"Doors open."

"Target Sierra 2. Fire one."

There is a thud, whoosh sound as the torpedo is fired.

John, "Sir, the Russians never opened their doors."

Cumberland smiles, "We are at war, XO. It's happening."

CONTROL, K-322 KASHALOT

Minin shouts, "Torpedo in the water! Another torpedo! Mark 48. It's the Los Angeles class."

Popov, "Calm. Who does it target?"

"Us, Captain."

"Ahead flank. Cavitate. Full down on the dive planes. Open the doors.

CONTROL, USS SAN FRANCISCO

"Conn, Sonar, The Russian is cavitating. They are changing depth."

The Captain's eyes are alight as he looks at the XO. Then Cumberland remembers he has the conn, "Understood Sonar. Will our fish hit?"

"I think so, sir."

CONTROL, K-322 KASHALOT

Popov, "Release the countermeasures."

"Countermeasures released." Four noise and bubble

generation canisters are released. They clear the screw and start building a wall between the torpedo and the fleeing submarine.

Popov, "Right full rudder."

The Mark 48 is a very advanced torpedo. It is fooled, but not for long.

They hear the torpedo sonar become muffled and then get loud again.

Popov lifts the microphone, "Brace for impact..." The torpedo hits under the engine room. The huge explosion bucks the submarine upward into a nose down attitude. The engine room crew are all killed instantly. The water tight doors at each end of the tunnel through the reactor hold. The submarine settles to the stern as the normal lights are extinguished and the emergency lighting come on.

CONTROL, USS SAN FRANCISCO

They hear the faint rumble of distant explosions reverberate through the hull.

Captain, "What was that?"

"Conn, Sonar, the Stoddert has been hit multiple times. Sir, we also got the Russian."

CONTROL, K-322 KASHALOT

Popov orders, "Blow stern ballast."

The circuit survives and many of the air tanks

astern do open. The ballast tanks are badly damaged, though and leaking air.

The settling to stern slows, "Blow bow ballast."

CONTROL, USS SAN FRANCISCO

Cumberland, "Is he sinking?"

Brown in Sonar, "Yes, sir. I can hear it venting air and steam, even over the Stoddert."

Cumberland looks up, smiles slightly, then slowly closes his fists and takes a deep breath. He notices Morrison watching and schools his face.

Morrison, "What is happening with the Stoddert?"

Brown, "She's been hit, sir. I think, three times. Her engines have stopped. I can hear steam venting. She is likely a goner, sir."

Morrison, "The other sub?"

Brown, "Also hit. The seas are getting noisy, sir."

Morrison, "I understand."

The captain moves to the chart table, "Morrison, do we have anything else out there?"

John joins him at the chart table, "Not that I know of, sir." He looks over the table that has the location, course and speed of all known contacts.

CONTROL, K-322 KASHALOT

The upward angle of the Russian boat's is getting

steeper. Starshina First Class Isaev says, "We are no longer sinking, sir. Depth is 200 meters and slowly rising."

Popov, "Understood. Release the rescue buoy."

Lebedev quietly asks, "Can we make it, sir?

CONTROL, USS SAN FRANCISCO

Brown, "Conn, Sonar, it looks like the Long Beach is slowing to render aid to the Stoddert. The Vinson is continuing south at high speed."

Cumberland pushes the button, "Anything else out there?"

"Not that we know. There are still reverberations from all the explosions. It will be a while before the ocean quiets down."

"Do your best, Brown." He smiles, holding the button down, "We are at war."

CONTROL, K-322 KASHALOT

Popov answers his crewman, "I don't know. Auxiliary Machinery, engage the high-pressure compressor and align it to fill the aft ballast tanks."

"Yes, Captain."

Popov, "Shift all possible weight forward. Flood all torpedo tubes."

The crew scrambles to follow his orders.

SONAR, USS SAN FRANCISCO

ST 1 Brown listens intently as he studies the water-fall. It is a mess. He starts to hear a faint rapid pulse, "Conn, Sonar, The Russian just turned on an air compressor. It looks like they are struggling to surface."

Cumberland bolts into Sonar, "You said it was dead."

Brown, "It is a mortal blow, sir. We hit its engine room. They are blowing ballast and trying to surface to abandon ship."

Cumberland reverses and storms into control, "Do we have a firing solution on tube two!"

John, "Sir?"

"They are trying to surface."

John's eyes open, then tighten. Quietly, "A word, sir."

The two men stare at each other.

"The firing solution for tube two is updated."

John, "Sir, the boat is dead. Firing again would be murder."

Cumberland, still staring at Morrison, "Maintain that solution."

CHAPTER 9

CONTROL, K-322 KASHALOT

The boat stops rising at 160 meters, then slowly starts slipping backwards, "Drop the anchor and set plans at full rise."

The rattle of the chain unwinding is deafening in the quiet boat. It seems to go on forever then there is a loud bang of the chain stop letting go. This lightens the boat but it comes from the front of the boat. It tilts up more and the slide downward increases. All the crew is forward hanging on where they can. They clearly hear the captain in the silence, "It has been an honor to serve with each and all of you. Lord, to you I command my soul."

A weld fails in the torpedo room. The pressure in the boat increases to thousands of pounds in less than a second. Everyone is incinerated where they stand. The crumpled boat sheds parts as it falls to the ocean floor 15,000 feet below.

CONTROL, USS SAN FRANCISCO

"Conn, Sonar, the Russian boat crushed. They are

gone."

Cumberland is silent, so John pushes the button, "Thank you Brown." John stands, hands behind his back and face neutral, "Orders, sir?"

"The war goes on. Come to 175. Make our speed ahead full. Let's get ahead of the fleet."

Morrison, "Sir, should we check in? We just killed a Russian boat."

Cumberland looks at Morrison a long moment, "Very well. XO, you have the conn. I have a message to write."

John turns toward the crew, "One degree up bubble. Make our depth 150 feet."

Backes joins him, whispering, "I'm not hallucinating? We just killed a Russian nuke boat?"

"We did. They were acting aggressively and the Captain was within his orders."

"Jesus Christ, man. Our families. This means it has gone up. He didn't even address the crew about it."

John nods his head slowly, "It is his call. I have the conn. Go aft and start talking to people. We did what we have trained for, sure, but we also killed about 100 sailors. We need to know how the crew is dealing."

"Yes, sir."

XO'S STATEROOM, USS SAN FRANCISCO

2321, DECEMBER 20st, 1941

John walks in from the shower and plops down on his chair, exhausted. He looks at his bed, then the paperwork on his desk, and decides to pull out the next letter from Lisa.

My Love,

This letter is for week two. I really hope your week has been good. I'm writing this as you lay sleeping in the next room and my heart swells with happiness. I need to share with you just what flavor of an idiot you just married. I remember like it was yesterday that day, 21 March, 1975. We had dinner on your father's ship. It was a destroyer named Coontz, which I thought was an odd name. Eleven times you had asked me to marry you.

I was an idiot. I couldn't see how I could be a Navy wife and a member of Metalsmith. Your mom tried to encourage me. She said she would help me with everything. Have I said your parents are awesome? They are. I had just got back from Metalsmith's first European tour. My song, 'Speaking to The Man,' was at number two. Our second album had just gone gold.

I saw marriage as a picket fence and the loss of my identity. PTA and hair turning grey. I should have said yes to your proposal that night, but I was an idiot. I cried. I ran. I am profoundly sorry. I will spend some time with your folks while you're gone.

Your mom and I can plan the big wedding.

Two days later in an Atlantic City hotel, all alone, I wrote the song below.

A gentle stroll along the beach,

Coffee hot and strong.

Another song another week,

And everything is wrong.

      Passing people all around, I must walk alone.

      Happiness a dreadful sound, I must walk alone.

      A lonely heart on a lonely shore,

      Seeking searching ever more.

      Hoping someday I might find

      Again, your heart to beat with mine.

I knew you were the one for me

The moment our eyes met.

You were the perfect melody.

We were the perfect set.

      Crowds of people push along, I must walk alone.

      Happiness a dreadful sound, I must walk

alone.

> A lonely heart on a lonely shore,
>
> Seeking searching ever more.
>
> Hoping someday I might find
>
> Again, your heart to beat with mine.

Seagulls make their lonely calls.

Walking in the sun,

I know I hurt you, hurt you babe,

Then all I did is run.

Trapped within these sandy walls

Face what I have done.

> Happiness a dreadful sound, I must walk
alone.

> In what way may I atone. Must I walk alone?
>
> A lonely heart on a lonely shore,
>
> Seeking searching ever more.
>
> Hoping someday I might find
>
> Again, your heart to beat with mine.
>
> Your heart to beat with mine.
>
> I need your heart with mine.

It is who I am. My pain is inflicted on my audience. I

like to think it helps them feel their own.

I love you dear heart. I will never ever walk away again.

Your Love,

Lisa

John lays his head on his desk and cries, wrenching, agonizing sobs, "It does."

0810, DECEMBER ENLISTED MESS, USS SAN FRANCISCO

DECEMBER 21st, 1941

Mallory and Wankowski are sharing a table as they listen to Nuclear training being conducted by LT Craig Cutting, the ELT Division officer. He is going over radiation distance and shielding math problems. The two are leaders of their divisions and know this shit by rote. To kill time, they are surreptitiously passing a notebook and playing tick tack toe.

Cumberland on the 1MC:

"Men of the San Francisco. I just received word from Admiral Ren. A research team on the carrier has determined the cause of the electrical event. Due to reasons at this time unknown, we and the battle-group were drawn back in time to December 19th, 1941. We are going to fight World War II. Gentlemen, I expect every one of you to rise up to the occasion. This is a fantastic opportunity to win the war for the good guys. That is all."

The mess decks erupt into conversations.

Mallory looks at his friend, "Mother fucker. He must be nuts."

Wankowski, "Did you hear the gleam in his voice. The blood thirsty bastard is looking forward to it. I think he gets off on killing."

The XO walks in on the pandemonium, "Quiet. Guys, quiet please."

They settle down, but the side conversations continue.

Morrison, "Questions?"

Miller raises his hand, "A million. First, is the Captain stoned or insane?"

Morrison, "The information is accurate. It has been verified. I've seen it myself."

Chief Hines, "How, sir?"

"We don't know."

Wankowski, "How do we get back, sir?"

"We don't know."

Mallory starts quietly cussing.

Wankowski, "What about our families?" The group grows quiet.

John takes a deep breath, "Most of our families have

not been born. We are going to have to be our family. Lord knows this sucks, but we do have a job to do. We have already lost a destroyer, and we nearly lost the carrier, because we didn't know what had happened. We also sank a Russian ship. In this war the Russians were our allies."

THE END

COMING NEXT

SHOULD ENGLAND FALL

BOOK FOUR

OF THE

FIGHTING TOMCATS

AND

PART TWO OF

SHARK AMONG THE MINNOWS

THE HUNTER/KILLER SERIES

OF THE

FIGHTING TOMCATS

ACKNOWLEDGEMENTS

We wish to thank ETNC(SW) Scott Richardson, Buckner F. Melton Jr., former submariners Andrew Brown, Craig Cutting, Greg Backes, RMC(SS) John

Barton, and all the submariners that helped us with this book. We would also like to thank all of our friends and family who are characters in this series. Thank you so much. Writing these books cannot be done without the support and help of our families and friends. There is not enough gratitude in the universe.

The views presented are those of the authors and do not necessarily represent the views of the DoD.

Email us at RoseHillPress17@gmail.com

Shark Among the Minnows

Book One, Part one of the Hunter/Killer Series: The Fighting Tomcats

First Edition

©2019 by Sofia R. Maki and Megan L. Maki

Cover design by Megan L. Maki

Photo courtesy of the U.S. Navy

MM1 Maki is a U.S. Navy veteran with twenty years of active service. MM1 Maki is a nuclear field machinist mate who served on the USS Carl Vinson, CVN-70, and two cruisers. During twelve years of sea time, MM1 Maki circumnavigated the earth once, transited the Panama Canal three times, served on the USS Carl Vinson during Enduring Freedom, and earned multiple campaign awards. S.R. Maki has a background in criminal justice and accounting.

Made in the USA
Coppell, TX
14 June 2023